Tropical Summer

Book Four

Tropical Breeze Series

Michele Gilcrest

Copyright © 2023 by Michele Gilcrest

All rights reserved.

No part of this book may be reproduced in any form or by any electronic or mechanical means, including information storage and retrieval systems, without written permission from the author, except for the use of brief quotations in a book review.

Chapter 1

Nora

Nora Emmerson followed the teleprompter as she covered the news for the most popular morning show on television. She'd done the job successfully over the past decade, working side by side with the country's top tier co-anchors. They ran the news desk like clockwork, broadcasting the latest headlines, delivering exactly what their listeners needed to hear. With a plush salary in the millions, backed by skyrocketing ratings, Nora was at the top of her game in her career. But, she often wished she could say the same about her love life — an area that proved to be distant, lonely and spiraling somewhat out of control.

On the exterior she always gave her viewers what they'd come to expect — big smiles, all the catchphrases, riveting news, and a great start to their day.

"And that concludes our morning show. Until next time, make it a great day, America." She smiled.

But internally there was turmoil lingering in the depths of her soul — a dark storm brewing and waiting to spill over.

Nora relaxed her cheeks at the signaling of her producer,

pushing herself away from the desk to head backstage. At the conclusion of each show it was customary for her to head to her dressing room, removing all the layers of t.v. makeup to allow her face to breathe. Today would be no different.

Clanking her three-inch heels down the hall alongside her assistant was a common occurrence. It was usually a time when they reviewed Nora's schedule for the following day. Except today had a bit of a different twist.

Passing Nora's electronic device, her assistant, Camille, began with the rundown. "Okay, looks like tomorrow starts off with your usual five a.m. meeting with Rhonda, then your normal prep for the show. Afterwards you have to record a promo, then that should wrap things up in the studio for the day. Oh, and by the way —" Camille braced herself in a grand way, causing Nora to pause.

"It looks like you landed an interview with none other than Fashion Forward magazine. They sent over a list of questions for you to review and want to know if you're free around noon tomorrow?"

Sighing, Nora pushed open her door. "That's almost comical if you ask me. Of all the people they can think of to interview, they choose a news anchor. My entire wardrobe is arranged by my stylist. Everybody knows if it weren't for the show I wouldn't look nearly as good."

"Nora, clearly they don't see it that way. I don't think you give yourself enough credit. You take fashion to another level. It's not the clothing in itself, but how you wear it. Besides, they didn't want anybody else. They called to book an interview with you."

Interesting. It seemed like that was the story of Nora's life. She was thankful and humbled by it, but she was always surrounded by people who wanted her for one thing or another. Interviews, meetings, photo ops, book signings, you name it.

Being pulled in a hundred different directions was common. However, the one who should desire to be with her most was usually busy catching flights or taking meetings — being attentive to everything and everybody except his very own wife.

Nora scoffed at the idea. "Trust me, the only thing they want is to make their magazine look good. Everybody knows how this business works. If you're popular, everybody wants a piece of the action. The minute your fame starts to wane, they're onto the next best thing."

Camille frowned. "Jeesh, did somebody wake up on the wrong side of the bed this morning?"

"I'm sorry, Cam. I guess I've been in somewhat of a rut these days. Ignore me." In a sing-song voice, Nora continued, "I should be grateful and honored to do such an interview. Please call them back and tell them that noon works."

"There she is. That's the Nora Emmerson we all know and love." Camille smiled.

Again, all Nora had to do was what she did best. Tuck away her hurt, put on a great big smile for the public, and continue to rise to the top. She'd finesse her skills and please the crowd — even if deep down inside her personal life was suffering.

"Thank you, Camille." Nora winked. "Now, unless you have anything else for me I'm dying to remove all the layers off my face. If I hurry up, I think I have enough time to catch a Spin class."

"Actually, there's one more thing. While you were on air you received an overnight envelope marked urgent. It could be fan mail for all I know. I'm happy to take care of it if you'd like."

Nora stepped out of her heels and tied her hair up. "You can leave it on my dressing table. I could use a little fan mail to cheer me up."

"Really? Do you mind if I ask, or —"

She flopped down in her chair. "There's no point in getting into it. It's the same old story. Another busy week, another missed date night with the hubby. You know how it goes. I'm sure all we need is a little getaway this summer to help us unwind and reconnect," Nora replied, picking up the envelope, noticing no return address.

Camille clasped her hands together. "Oh, my gosh. I have the perfect idea. The girls upstairs have been raving about Harbour Island. They keep saying it's the perfect little getaway. How about I look into it, and you can surprise Liam with a romantic randevous for two? It would be lovely if you could get away for your birthday next week, but at least plan something for this summer."

Nora hesitated, glancing down at her watch. "I'd have to check with Liam or his secretary regarding his schedule. I'm sure he's heading to his regular Thursday afternoon appointment right now, but yeah sure, why not. Look into it for me. It might be just what we need to help revive things again."

Backing out of the room with two thumbs in the air, Camille replied, "Perfect. I'll get on it right away. This is going to be a trip to remember, I know it will."

Nora chuckled. "You're acting as if the trip is booked already."

"Think positively, Nora. As a visionary I can see these things before they come into existence. How many times have I told you — what you need is a vision board just like the one I have at home. Envisioning you and Liam on a romantic trip should be right there on your board along with winning your next award for best anchor of the year."

Nora began ripping the envelope open. "Good grief. Please, don't start with the vision board talk again. Although, I see nothing wrong with writing my goals down on my calendar,

I promised you I'd make a board and I will. Now — scoot so I can get dressed for spin class." She smiled.

"Good. I'll see you later." Camille waved.

Once Nora was alone, she shook her head, laughing at the idea. She wasn't much of a creative, cut and paste type. But, she did see the importance of making goals. And, like Camille suggested, her relationship definitely needed a fresh vision.

Nora reached into the envelope pulling out a large set of photos. At first glance it seemed meaningless. A picture showing the rear view of a couple, walking arm-in-arm into a famous hotel. *Nonsense.* She thought.

Except the words written at the bottom of the photo caused her to utter aloud as she read, *Thursday meetings.*

Gasping at the next picture, Nora could hear her own breathing. As plain as day it was Liam pecking the woman on the cheek. Barely able to see straight, she read the words, *The same place, the same time, every single week.*

If this was some sort of sick prank a fan was playing on her it certainly wasn't funny. Looking back at the first photo, she recognized the Park Avenue address. She'd seen it a thousand times, and recognized it as a place where they'd stopped for cocktails and dinner. But — the woman with him. Who was she?

"This is stupid," she said aloud. Liam wouldn't be so dumb as to walk in public locking arms with another woman, knowing how easily he could be spotted. He was smarter than that. Plus, his wife was seen every morning on televisions across the country over several news stations. Everybody knew who she was, therefore by association, everybody knew who he was. *This had to be a hoax.*

Of course, curiosity had the best of her as she flipped to the third photo. This time she could make out the two of them laughing, while facing each other at an elevator. It was Liam alright — with his salt and pepper, neatly trimmed haircut and custom-tailored suit. His body looked fit for a magazine and she could recognize it anywhere. The woman, on the other hand, had a distinct mole beside her nose and looked absolutely stunning.

The last picture was probably the worst of them all. Located in what appeared to be a hotel hallway was a photo of the backside of Liam walking hand-in-hand with the same woman. The words at the bottom were plainly written, *Thursdays at noon. Room 226.* Signed, *from one scorned woman to another.*

Scorned woman? Nora fought back the rising feeling in her stomach causing her mouth to salivate. Her first instinct was to rip the photos in half and fling them across the room. But, that wouldn't resolve anything. Instead she remained in her chair, feeling physically numb. Her mind wasn't numb though. It was far from it, as she mentally recalled various conversations they'd had as of late.

First, there was the dinner date he'd canceled, stating something about having to work late. But that happened so many times, she sort of grew used to it. Then, there was the last minute trip to go see his parents in Connecticut. Actually, several spontaneous trips to go see his parents. But, he'd always been a mama's boy, so she didn't really think much of that either. Plus, in his defense they were growing older and in need of extra care.

Wait. Why am I trying to justify his actions? she wondered.

If nothing else made sense, one thing did. These pictures were real. Unless fabricated in order to make Liam look bad, he looked awfully familiar with the mystery woman in the photos. And the only way she'd confirm if these Thursday hotel meetings were real was to go and see for herself.

Once the salivating stopped, she shoved the images back in

the express envelope and gripped the edge of her seat.

"A car. That's it. I'll call for a car to drive me to the hotel, confirm this is nothing but a joke, then head to the gym," she said aloud.

As Nora feverishly leapt out of her chair to change clothes all kinds of thoughts ran through her mind. For instance, who was the woman scorned and what was she so mad about? And, if this was any indicator of the condition of her marriage to Liam, then they were in way more trouble than Nora suspected.

Stop. she thought. This is insane. They'd been married for over twenty-five years. Yeah, sure, they had their rough patches every now and then, but who didn't? They'd been through everything together. During year five they were told they wouldn't be able to have kids — but the marriage remained strong. During year ten he survived a nearly debilitating car accident — the marriage still remained strong. And, ten years ago to date, her career took off, skyrocketing her to the top of the charts as a news anchor. Again — the marriage had always remained strong. So, why on earth should she respond to photos from a likely jealous viewer who probably digitally manipulated a fake encounter at a hotel?

I'm not going. I'll calmly sit down with him tonight over dinner and find a way to gently bring this up.

Nora walked over to the sink where she normally removed her television makeup, leaning over for what felt like a full minute. Flashbacks of the pictures ran through her mind as she stared down the drain. *Thursdays at noon. Room 226.*

The impulse to head to the hotel may have been suppressed, but there was no rule that said she couldn't call just to be certain. A scroll through her contacts is all it would take, then she'd make a quick call, rule out the foolishness and then carry on with her day.

She dialed the prestigious hotel and was greeted by an attendant.

With her heart racing a mile a minute, she did the unthinkable and lied. "Good morning, this is Liam Emmerson's secretary calling. Mr. Emmerson is hosting a meeting at the hotel this morning, and I'd like to have important files that he requested sent over. Unfortunately, he failed to confirm the room number with our mail carrier. Would you mind looking it up for me?"

Listening intently, she repeated after the person on the other end of the line. "Mm, hm. Just to confirm that was room 226, correct? Okay, thank you." She gulped, then hung up.

Nora squeezed her eyes shut to drown out the imagery of an affair in her mind. *Liam wouldn't.* Therefore, there had to be an explanation. He simply wouldn't do it. Not to her, not to their marriage, or to their reputation.

Nora picked up the phone again, this time dialing Denise, his secretary. Putting on her most melodious voice she said, "Hi, it's Nora. How are you?" She waited. "I'm fine, thank you. I was wondering if you could help me —"

She stopped mid-sentence, realizing this might not be a good idea. Denise was Liam's right-hand woman, bailing him out of numerous work situations, serving as his confidante and informant. If anyone were to ever give him a heads up about anything, it would be Denise.

"You know what, Denise. I'm so sorry. You'll have to forgive me. I thought I tapped a button to call my hair salon and somehow I accidentally called you instead. As if you're not busy enough as it is." She fake chuckled.

Breathing a sigh of relief after catching her mistake, Nora exchanged a few pleasantries, then concluded the call.

By this point it was inevitable, Nora was either going to dial for her car service to take her to spin class, or she'd request to head straight to the hotel. Either way, a simple text message to the car service could ultimately decide her fate.

At the hotel, three hard knocks on door number two-twenty-six was all it took to hear Liam's voice roar "who is it?" from the inside. He was prompt and responsive — and certainly didn't sound like a man who was in the middle of an affair — a reassuring thought to Nora.

As nerve-wracking as it was to lie and gain access upstairs, Nora had to do it. She was raised among a family of investigators, and she was a journalist for goodness' sake. Besides, how else could she remove those haunting images from her mind? Now, all she had to do was pretend she was coming over to surprise him, bringing an end to the stupid hoax, just as she'd suspected. *The things people can do with digital images these days.*

"Room service," she said in a ridiculous voice, just to throw him off. Liam would never suspect in a million years that she'd be on the other side of the door. For ten years, she'd operated like clockwork, following her before dusk routine at the studio, squeezing in a ton of work in between and concluding the day with a workout of some sort. Being free so early in the day was rare, but if this is what it took to put her mind at ease, she was all for it.

Nora slid her shades above her head and stood out of view. While listening to the sound of the lock turn, her nerves rattled.

Shock waves traveled through Nora's veins when she took in the sight that emerged from the room. It was nothing at all like what she'd hoped for; instead, it was every faithful woman's nightmare.

Chapter 2

Meg and Samuel

"Dad, it means so much to have you here, sharing this special occasion with Parker and I." Meg smiled.

"Are you kidding? A beautiful wedding ceremony with my baby girl as the bride. Mariam and I wouldn't miss it for anything in the world."

Meg's wedding would kick off the summer season at the main house of Seaside B&B in one week. Her friend, Frankie's wedding would be held at the second and newly renovated house, just one month later. To think, it was just a year ago when the whole plan was discussed — and now it was really happening.

Meg strolled alongside her father in the sand. "I'm glad Parker and I waited. We wanted to do this right, inviting our family and friends to take part and allowing you and Parker the opportunity to spend time together."

Samuel stopped, picking up a seashell along the way. "You don't know how much that means to me. Back home it's been all about figuring out how to manage all this extra time on my hands now that I'm finally retired. If it's not that, then it's more doctors appointments, and just life in general. But, coming out here and spending time with you guys has definitely been a nice change of pace. I'm only sorry we couldn't make it out here sooner."

Meg watched the formation of crow's feet form around her dad's eyes as he tried to smile. That plus the subtle air about him that didn't go unnoticed. He was great at pretending to be strong whenever something weighed on his mind. At least he thought he was — but Meg always knew better.

"Dad, is everything okay? You don't seem like yourself lately."

He looked away. "Everything's fine, sweetheart."

"You know you can tell me, whatever it is. I can handle it. I'm not the little girl you used to put on a big smile for, while pretending like everything was okay."

He chuckled. "Goodness. I'm good, Meg. Really, I am." The laughter faded. "You know what — you're just like your mother, worrying about everyone but yourself, even during your wedding week. Boy, how I wish she could be here to share this moment."

Uncertain of whether to believe him or not, she just listened.

"If your mother were still living she'd be so thrilled she wouldn't know what to do with herself. I can see her running around, helping with arrangements and doing all the things a proud mother would do."

Meg nodded. "She'd probably ask what took me so long to find the right man. Waiting until nearly forty-six years old to get married wasn't exactly in the plans."

Her dad's expression faded as he tossed the seashell back in the sand. "I'm certain we could say that about a lot of things in life. I can think of so many instances where life didn't go according to plan. But, none of that matters. In this case, age is just a number — remember that. The only thing that's important is you're marrying the right guy. Someone who'll take care of you for the rest of your days together. Somebody who will take care of you even after I'm long gone."

As they strolled, Meg flashed back to her days of trying on her mother's fancy shoes and playing dress up with her cosmetics. Unfortunately, those memories weren't as crystal clear as they used to be. Her mother had passed away when Meg was young, leaving her with distant memories, occasional dreams that weren't as frequent as they used to be, and a few photo albums.

Her dad perked up. "So, have you got your dress all ready to go? Any last-minute errands that Mariam and I can assist you with?"

"Yes, you can assist with helping me to stay calm as a cucumber throughout the entire process. I don't know why Parker and I thought we could manage running the B&B in the midst of our wedding week. But, nevertheless, it's happening. Fingers crossed it won't turn out to be a disaster."

In reality, Meg knew they had every plan in place to see to it that everything ran smoothly. Ms. Brown had been hired to oversee all things related to housekeeping, Chef Sean would continue dazzling their guests with selections from the kitchen, and their new assistant manager, Corrine, would see to it that the guests were cared for and happy.

She glanced at her father who appeared to be lost in thought. "You've always been a pro at keeping me calm — right, Dad?"

"Hm," he said, seeming distant. "Oh, yes. Right dear. Anything you need, we've got it covered."

It wasn't exactly the usual response Meg had come to expect from her father. But, it was a busy time for everyone, and perhaps in his case, jet lag was finally settling in.

She continued, "Casey is flying in tomorrow with the family. It's going to be nice having her here after not seeing her in so long."

"I'll bet, honey," he responded. "You guys have known each other since you were little. It's fitting that she would be here to support you on your special day."

Meg watched as her father paused to hold the side of his temple.

"Are you okay, Dad?" she asked.

"Don't mind me. Every once in a while I suffer from these headaches. According to the doctor, my caffeine addiction doesn't help. I've been working on it, but sometimes it gets the best of me. Not to worry, I'll take something when I get back to the room."

"Are you sure? We can head back now if you'd like," Meg pressed.

"It's fine — really."

Watching him continue to squint, she began to say, "Dad, I really think you should —"

"Meg!" he snapped. "I said, I'm fine."

She paused, feeling the sting from his quick response. Again, it wasn't his norm, but who knew how to define normal these days? With the miles between them, she could tell so much had changed.

"Meg, forgive me. You're right. I guess with traveling and hitting the ground running, I'm more tired than expected. I should go — perhaps if I rest for an hour or two it will make all the difference."

She placed her hand on his back. "Sure, Dad."

* * *

Later that evening, Samuel sifted feverishly through his travel bag, trying to ensure everything was in place. It had become a part of his nightly routine, no different than bathing and brushing his teeth. With his medication in place, he could count on a good night's rest.

"Mariam, where's my pills?" He sighed. "I arranged my luggage just so— putting everything in a place where I could easily find it when I returned. Have you been rummaging through my things? I can't find what I'm looking for to save my life."

"Sam — I'm certain wherever it is we will find it. I'll help you look. In the meantime, you're about to miss a beautiful view of the sunset. Why don't you pull up a chair on the balcony, dear."

The two had been joined at the hip for better or worse for over twenty years. She had a loving connection with her step-daughter, Meg, and a heart of gold for Samuel through all their ups and downs. Unfortunately, little did they know some of their biggest challenges still lay ahead.

He flung his toothbrush into the sink. "The sun will rise and set again tomorrow. But, if I don't take my medication, I'll be too much of a wreck to enjoy it. How pathetic would it look for me to show up to my daughter's wedding with bags under my eyes, feeling too tired to keep up."

Mariam leaned against the counter, holding his toiletry bag in hand. "Sam, I'm not sure what's gotten into you lately, but I can assure you everything is going to be okay. Here we are staying at this beautiful B&B, surrounded by family, the trade winds, tropical sunsets, and all you can seem to obsess about is your medication. Maybe you forgo the pills for a little while, honey. Maybe you can ease up a bit — just until we get back to New York to see Dr. Rosenburg.

Ease up? he thought. It's the last thing he could do. Of course, he wouldn't expect Mariam to understand. Besides, sleepless nights were the least of his problems. The layers of turmoil that troubled his thoughts ran deep, disturbing his consciousness as he tried to sleep at night. The burden was way more than he was willing to admit to anyone or even face for himself.

In a calm voice he replied, "Mariam, I'll be fine. I just need to ensure I get a few hours in, so I can be bright-eyed and present for Meg as we prepare to escort her down the aisle. You can understand that, can't you?"

"I — I suppose."

According to the way Sam thought, it wouldn't be fair to burden Mariam with the truth of his internal battles. The struggles that kept him up during the night was his journey to overcome, not hers.

She dug into his bag one last time. "Darlin', the bottle was right here all along," she said, handing it over to him. She stepped closer, clasping his hand in hers. "Sam, please make me a promise."

He looked up.

"Promise me these pills won't become a crutch. I know it's not easy for you to open up and talk about the things that are on your mind. But, I want you to be healthy, honey. I want you to be here with me for as long as God will allow."

The warmth of her touch eased the tension in his body. He leaned in, kissing her ever so gently on the forehead. "There's no need to worry, my love. Everything is just fine."

The words sounded good at least, even if he knew it wasn't true. It was his story and he was sticking to it until it became his reality. Coming from generations of men who were fix-it-your-selfers, Samuel didn't know how to ask for help. He only knew how to push through as best as he could— maybe even withhold a few things until the time was right. He'd do anything to protect his family from what he was hiding.

Chapter 3

Nora

"I - I'm looking for Liam," Nora exclaimed. She locked eyes with the stunning woman with the mole, but her eyes soon drifted down, noticing her half removed, disheveled clothing. It was clear she'd been in a hurry to disrobe because her present look was unsuitable for a company meeting. As if feeling ashamed, the woman modestly began tucking in her blouse.

Nora could feel the heat rising in her neck like a hot furnace. But, it wasn't until Liam approached, wearing an unbuttoned business shirt that she totally lost her cool.

"What in the hell are you doing?" she lashed out.

He downplayed it. "Nora, please. I can explain."

She watched as the woman looked up to Liam with the eyes of a lost puppy dog, and said, "I should go."

You're darn right you should go. You shouldn't have been *here in the first place,* Nora thought. But, just when she thought things couldn't get any worse, it was what Liam did next that surprised her.

"Give me a few minutes. Wait for me inside." He motioned.

Watching the woman take one last glance into her eyes, then disappear back into the suite was enough to make Nora want to spit. She proceeded to step forward, but he shifted his body, blocking the entrance way.

"What are you doing?" she asked, observing his calm demeanor, which ticked her off even more. None of this made sense. Here she was thinking he'd been an upstanding husband while all along he apparently was having weekly rendezvous that didn't involve her. And, what did he mean by give me a few minutes — wait for me inside? *Had he missed the memo?* He was busted. The photographic whistle blower was right. This is the part where the mistress was supposed to storm off — never to be seen again and he was supposed to beg for her forgiveness.

"Answer me, Liam."

"I don't know where to begin," he said.

"You can begin by explaining to me why you have a —" She paused in haste. Nora could think of a thousand words to use but none of them would be kind, not that it mattered. "Why is she in your room delivering everything but business, during your so-called business meeting?"

He cupped his face, then slid his hands down his beard. "I didn't want you to find out like this."

"What!"

He shushed her, drawing the door semi-closed as he looked up and down the hall.

"Have you lost your mind? Don't shush me. I'm your wife, not her!"

"I've been meaning to bring this up to you for some time now. Just not in this way."

"Bring what up, Liam? The fact that you're having an affair? Well, you're too late," she said, digging into her bag.

Nora held up the photos to prove her point. "Somebody out there did the job for you, ensuring that I'd know exactly where to find you during your so-called Thursday meeting. The sad part is, you have absolutely no regard — not only for our marriage, but apparently no regard for my career. I'd be shocked if these photos don't end up splattered all over the newspapers by the morning."

He exhaled, rolling his eyes at the sight of the revealing pictures. But, sadly, it didn't change his mind. "I'm not sure who's behind the photos. I'll call Laura this afternoon and ask her to reach out to a few of my contacts. We'll ensure that they don't get out there and into the wrong hands."

As she stood there listening to him transitioning into business mode, which is what he always did best, it was actually mind-boggling to hear. Had he missed the fact that the pictures were already in her hands? Had he misunderstood that she was standing at the threshold of his lies?

"This is ludacris," she said, allowing the photos to hang by her waist. "I'm still standing here waiting to hear your explanation and all you can manage to do is reference your connections and contacts. I'm so angry, I could send these pictures to the newspaper myself, just so I can ruin your life. Now — start telling me what I came to hear or else I may strongly consider it."

Holding his hands out, he hurriedly spoke. "Let's be rational, Nora. Leaking those pictures wouldn't exactly be a positive reflection on you."

"Speak!"

He took a deep breath. "Okay. You and I have been distant for a while now. It's no one's fault, but we both have high profile careers, pulling us in different directions. It was inevitable that something like this would happen."

She cut him a sharp look. "After twenty-five years? Really? This wasn't inevitable. You invited her into your life."

That's when it dawned on Nora — the seductress woman inside his suite hadn't been the only one. The photos were signed *from one scorned woman to another,* meaning there were more.

She pointed to the signature line. "You son of a —. You've been having one affair after the other, haven't you?"

"Nora, please. I know this is hard to hear, but I may as well come out with it. We're getting married. Not before I file, of course. But, we're on that path. The two of us make sense together. We're in the same industry — we speak each other's language."

"Stop. Stop it right now! You're standing here telling me, with total disregard to twenty-five long years of marriage, that it's over?" She paused, rendering him speechless. "You couldn't find the decency to approach me about marriage counseling, or anything, to see if we could make things work? Are you kidding me?"

She could feel something the size of a miniature golf ball welling on the inside of her throat. Mixed-up feelings of embarrassment and rage possessed her body as it was all becoming clear. The stunning woman in his room was staying, and Nora was receiving a pink slip.

"Nora, when was the last time we made love?"

Her instincts kicked in, causing her to fling the photos at him. "If that's the only substance you're made of, then you can have your filthy little affair. I wouldn't be surprised if you didn't lose her the same way you got her."

Realizing where this was going she turned about-face, and proceeded to leave. Then she stopped. "Hey, Liam," she said, as she turned around observing him picking the pictures off the floor.

With every step she took back in his direction, she finagled her rare, precious stone and removed it from her finger.

As he fixated on the ring, she placed it in her purse and snatched the photos that he retreated from the floor. "Thanks. I'm sure these will be useful to me in court when I prove how much of a liar and a cheat you are."

She then walked off, sliding her sunglasses down her face and then flipped him the bird.

* * *

"Camille, I need you to cancel tomorrow's interview with Fashion Forward. Actually, I need you to clear out my entire calendar for the next two weeks."

Nora Emmerson could not get her mind past the look on Liam's mistress' face when she opened the door. There was no mistaking the woman knew exactly who Nora was. She was only the face of the country's most favorite morning news show. A face that could not be mistaken.

She sat in front of a bottle of wine feeling numb all over. Liam's blatant disregard for their marriage and willingness to live a lie made her sick to the pit of her stomach. He'd successfully convinced her that the last two decades of their lives had been a total waste, easily leaving a sour taste in her mouth. Now, at fifty, for a woman who always had it together — she felt lost. Unable to think straight. Unable to hold it together for the morning news.

"Uh, surely you don't mean that. Management doesn't have you slated for a vacation until later this summer. Speaking of vacation, you're not going to believe what I discovered about Harbour Island."

"Camille."

"Yes?"

"Forget Harbour Island. Forget anything having to do with the trip and anything having to do with Liam Emmerson for that matter. If he tries to reach out to you, tell him I'm not accepting his calls."

"Okayyy. You're making me nervous, Nora. Is everything okay?"

Taking a deep breath, Nora replied, "No. Everything is not okay, but it will be. I just need you to clear my calendar and let management know I'm taking a leave of absence."

"For how long?"

"Two weeks... three weeks. Who knows? Enough time to clear my mind," *and file for a divorce.* The last part she thought of instinctively but reserved the comment instead of sharing.

"You're making me worried, Nora. This is so unlike you. How am I going to answer questions should they ask? No, when they ask is more like it."

Nora stared at the bottle before reaching for an opener. "This is why they have other anchors, Camille. They're all waiting for their next opportunity to fill the top slot. As far as I'm concerned you can let them have at it. If I don't take time off, I'll be of no use to the show anyway."

"Am I allowed to ask?"

Nora closed her eyes, allowing the first tear to drop since she'd left the hotel. "I can't go into great detail, other than I'm sure you'll start to hear about it on social media soon. Until then, just think of the worst possible thing a man could do in a marriage, and I'm sure you'll come up with the right answer." She sighed.

"I'm sorry, Nora."

"Don't be," she responded, replaying various scenes from the day's events in her mind over and over again. The one that stood out the most was the moment Liam shifted in the doorway, as if protecting his mistress against the woman he was supposed to love.

Camille interrupted her train of thought. "Look, you know I have your back, which means if there's anything — and I mean anything you need me to do, just say the word."

In a monotone voice Nora replied, "Thanks, Camille."

"There's no need to thank me. I only hope you get revenge, making him pay for all the hurt and pain that I hear in your voice."

Nora let out a dry laugh. "Revenge." It wasn't exactly top on her list of ways to treat people. However, today Liam had given her something to think about.

"You've always said that one of your favorite ways to relax is to draw a hot bubble bath. Why don't you do that tonight, then lie down and try to get some rest. I'm going to text to check on you in the morning."

"I'll be fine. It's nothing that a bottle of wine and maybe a visit to my shrink won't cure," Nora replied sarcastically. All along, the tears continued flowing down her face.

"It doesn't matter. I'm checking on you anyway. Have a good night, Emmerson."

Nora paused for a long moment, realizing she no longer wanted any association with the name. She now detested the name Emmerson, even if it was a part of her public persona.

"Maxwell."

Camille replied, "What was that?"

"The last name will soon be Maxwell. Nora B. Maxwell."

* * *

* * *

Riddled with thoughts that would keep her awake into the early hours of the morning, Nora maneuvered out of bed. Everything ached from her shoulders down to a sharp pain in her neck, making it difficult to turn her head. *Is this what life was going to be like?* she wondered. Sleepless nights filled with thoughts of the many times her husband had probably lied to her. Mapping out the past several months of disconnect between them, and the countless lonely nights. No — surely there was a better option than this.

Nora wandered through the halls of their Penthouse apartment, flicking on the kitchen lights. She figured maybe her favorite can of hazelnut coffee would make her feel better. Four powerful scoops of the dark roast was usually all it took, but this morning might call for five.

She glanced over the quartz countertop at a picture of the two of them at a banquet. *How phony,* she thought. All the smiles and laughter with champagne glasses in hand meant nothing when the life she was living was a lie. She turned the photo down and headed for the restroom instead.

In the mirror, she saw her raccoon eyes with swollen lids. It was the perfect reflection of how she felt. Sad, miserable, and with each passing hour even angrier.

Bent over the sink Nora lathered her face and even shed a few more tears as she did it. She'd given herself a pass to let it all hang out, feeling all the feels. And then, when the time was right she'd have her day in court. It still amazed her how Liam had managed to become so invested in this other woman — but who knows, maybe the affair had gone on much longer than she'd imagined.

She turned off the faucet and patted her face dry. In the mirror she could see a reflection of Liam's closet — that's when it hit her. Maybe there were clues that had been there all along, among his things, and she was just too busy to see it.

Exhaling, Nora flipped the light switch, scanning her eyes across all of his suits. Everything was aligned from business to casual, lightest to darkest color, with an exhaustive shoe collection. If one didn't know any better they'd think they landed in the men's section of a Manhattan department store.

Nora shuffled through his shirts, inspecting the collar of each one. She then dug her hands into the pockets of his suits, but stopped. *This is foolish. You already have pictures, what more do you need.* That's when she angrily turned around to leave, bumping into his laundry basket, tipping it over. Several striped golf shirts fell out, one with the distinct smell of a woman's perfume. *Go figure. I guess you expected the cleaning lady to keep your dirty little secrets.*

Back in the kitchen a text message buzzed from Camille.

How are you doing? I was worried about you last night.

Nora replied, *Regarding my well-being, I'm fine. Emotionally, I've seen better days.*

I'm so sorry, Nora.

Don't be. I know women who've been through worse. On another note, if you wouldn't mind, please keep an eye out for any additional important mail. If you come across anything, please set it aside for me.

Of course. Also, not speaking as your assistant, but as your confidante and friend, I'm calling this afternoon to book a reservation for you. Getting away may be just what you need to clear your mind and help you feel better. Unless you willfully call and cancel, your suite will be waiting for upi this weekend. Already called and spoke to the owner. They have room for you.

A beeping sound from the coffee machine reminded Nora that her fresh brew was ready.

She pulled out a mug, then picked up the cell phone to reply.

A reservation where?

Seaside B&B on Harbor Island. A flight leaves early Saturday morning out of Laguardia. When you get there, all you have to do is ask for the head manager, Corrine.

Nora poured a cup, then whirled her spoon around, mixing in the cream.

I can't just take off like that. There will be no one to look after things here at the apartment.

Was Liam thinking about the apartment (or you) when he left? Sorry, not trying to be crude, but the story was leaked overnight on social media.

Of course, that was exactly what Nora didn't need. An excuse for people to gawk at her as she walked down the streets of Manhattan. An excuse for everyone to look at her with pity.

She stood there, clasping her mug, not knowing how to respond.

Camille replied, *You don't have to answer that. Just know that the reservations are being made. If you cancel them, that's on you. If there's anything else I can do for you, please let me know.*

Nora drew in a deep breath and released with the words, *Thank you.*

Chapter 4

Meg

Drawing in oxygen from a brown paper bag had proven to be calming to Meg — even if it lasted for only a short while. "I think we might be in over our heads," she said, in between inhaling and exhaling.

It would take more than a gathering involving Parker, Frankie and her fiancé, David, to calm her down. Instead, it would take a solid plan, hope, a prayer, and even a miracle at this point.

Holding her meditation fingers in the air Frankie replied, "Breathe. There's nothing — and I mean nothing that can or will get in the way of you having the wedding you've always dreamed of." She then turned to her fiancé. "David and I are willing to do whatever it takes to help out, isn't that right, babe?"

"Of course. Just tell us whatever you need and consider it done. It's the least we can do, given that you guys are being so generous to let us have our wedding here," he replied.

Parker slid next to Meg on the couch in the guests' parlor, stroking the back of her hair. "Meg, you know I'd move mountains for you if I could. But, in order to help you have to start by talking to me. Tell me what's wrong, sweetheart."

Meg relaxed her arm, releasing the paper bag to her lap. "I guess the real question is what's right. I knew we were taking on a lot this week with our family in town, and the wedding. Having so much going on while still running the B&B is a lot, but I was confident with Corrine on the team that we could handle it. But now — with the phone call that just came in. This might be the very thing that puts us over the edge."

Frankie's eyes widened. "The suspense is killing me, already. I can't think of one thing that could possibly go wrong within a week of your wedding."

Meg replied, "Well, I can. For starters, I just received a phone call from Camille Sanchez requesting to book one of our suites for the next fourteen days." She emphasized.

David shrugged his shoulders. "Okay, so that's one extra guest on the roster, providing you and Parker with enough money to pay for a dreamy honeymoon by the end of the summer. What's so terrible about that?"

With all eyes focused in Meg's direction she stood up and began staring out the window. "If only it were that simple. Camille happens to be the assistant calling on behalf of our very first celebrity guest, Nora Emmerson."

Parker leapt out of his seat. "The — Nora Emmerson? As in America's morning news anchor, Nora Emmerson?"

"Yes. As in — a woman who's accustomed to receiving five-star service and having people at her beck and call, Nora Emmerson."

When Meg turned around she could see Frankie covering her mouth, trying to contain herself. "Nora Emmerson is staying here? Oh...man... I've always dreamt of being a famous television personality, but I can settle for meeting one face-to-face."

David nudged Frankie, drawing her back to the heart of the matter. "Sorry Meg, carry on," Frankie said.

"Her assistant explained that Ms. Emmerson will be here on a much-needed break and her arrival is to be kept quiet. If folks on the island end up discovering her as she's out and about, that's one thing — but otherwise she's expecting a quiet stay at the B&B with round the clock service and no interruptions."

Parker chimed in. "When will she arrive?"

"Tomorrow morning, one week from our wedding day to be precise. I don't know what I was thinking," she said, then began breathing in her paper bag again.

"Oh boy," Parker sighed.

The surmounting pressure was enough to make Meg feel faint. Yet, something made her press forward the same way one would on an adrenaline high that couldn't be controlled.

She continued, "Honestly, I'm starting to question my sanity at this point. When Camille revealed who she was calling for, I panicked, saying yes before I could think straight. Hosting Nora Emmerson at our B&B could really help boost business for us. That part is a no-brainer. But, the timing couldn't be more terrible."

Reaching for the back of his head, Parker exhaled. "We'll make it work. Trust me, if it were me on the other end of that line, I would've done the same thing. Asking her to pick another date probably would've been a major turn off, sending her elsewhere and leaving us with regrets. This is a once in a lifetime opportunity and we really need to take it."

Flopping her hands to her side, Meg replied, "Yes, but are we going to regret not having a larger staff to handle this? Chef Sean and Corrine can only do so much without us."

David interrupted, "I have an idea. Why don't you allow Frankie and I to take on a couple of shifts the day of your ceremony. I know my way around the kitchen if Chef Sean needs an extra hand and Frankie can be on standby, ready to take any requests should Ms. Emmerson call the front desk."

Across the room, Meg could see the gleam in Frankie's eyes. Of course, it wasn't exactly realistic to send a super fan with minimal experience to personally cater to Ms. Emmerson's every need.

Frankie clasped her hands together. "Maybe I can get her to sign one of my t-shirts while serving her favorite cocktail."

Again, Meg chimed in. "Or — maybe I should've exercised a little common sense and declined the offer. I don't know what's worse — saying no to the most famous guest the B&B has ever had, or saying yes and realizing we can't handle the job. I can almost see the headlines in the local papers now, boasting terrible ratings after Ms. Emmerson publicly blasts how much of an epic fail we are."

"Meg," Parker said. He rested his arms on her shoulders and stared her square in the eyes.

"Yes?"

"We are not going to be an epic fail. Together, we are Seaside B&B. This place has a long standing history — born from the love and hospitality that Old Man Barnes and his wife created. We made a decision to carry on their legacy — remember?"

"Yes," she replied with moisture welling up in her eyes.

He continued, "Good. Then we'll figure this out. We'll see to it that Nora Emmerson has an unforgettable experience. And, we'll see to it that you and I still have an amazing wedding. Understood?"

Meg nodded, but still harbored a high level of uncertainty.

* * *

That evening Meg dusted around the lamps and bed post of the Seabreeze Suite. It was one of their most private and relaxing rooms tucked away in the back of the B&B with its own ocean view.

With everything in place, she folded a white towel in the shape of a dove and left a welcome card in front of it.

Just like so, she thought. Then she exited the room. According to Meg's planning, the Seabreeze would be the room Ms. Emmerson stayed in, and Parker's family from out of town would occupy the rooms upstairs.

Down the hall, Meg raised her fist to knock on her dad's door, when overhearing a heated exchange stopped her in her tracks.

"Sam. I'm not arguing with you about this. When we get back to New York you will make an appointment to see Dr. Rosenburg, and if you don't, I'm making it for you. Passing out in a drunken state while consuming sleeping pills is hardly acceptable. I don't care how much trouble you're having with falling asleep. I won't stand for it anymore."

Meg slipped her hand over her mouth, knowing she should walk away, but instead listened as they continued to argue.

"Mariam, lower your voice for God's sake. You're making too much of this as always."

There was a pause. Then Mariam replied, "Oh, really? Am I, Sam? Or are you in denial that you may have a problem that's beyond your control? I'm trying to help you before this thing spirals, getting worse than it already is."

Thinking for a moment, Meg wondered if their argument had anything to do with the way her father behaved on the beach the other day.

"I'm going to be frank with you, Sam. You've been drinking too much and you're hooked on those sleeping pills as if your life depended on it. Is this really the way you want to live your life? After all the years of planning to finally be retired, and to spend more time with your daughter and your loved ones. If you keep this up, you won't be around to enjoy it. Sam — honey. If only you would talk to me and tell me what's causing you to act this way."

Meg stepped back from the door, swallowing quietly. In all her years of being raised by her father she never saw him struggle. The hardest thing he'd ever dealt with to her knowledge was the passing of her mother when she was a young girl — and even then there was no alcohol and no sleeping pills. Just lonely nights with heart-wrenching cries from his bed to ease the pain. It was something they both shared.

She heard Mariam speak. "Sam. Say something."

"What is there to say, Mariam? It sounds like you have it all figured out. According to you I have a problem and I need to go see Dr. Rosenburg. So, fine. I'll go see him. But, what's he going to do? Check me out from head to toe and tell me nothing is wrong other than I have trouble sleeping. Heck, he may even tell me I need more exercise, or I need to lose more weight. Whatever he has to say, I'll listen, but only to appease you. Now, if you'll excuse me, Mariam, I'm going for a walk. I need a breath of fresh air."

Meg darted around the corner, quickly entering another empty guest room.

* * *

With her head resting on the closed door, Meg closed her eyes, listening to the sound of her father passing by. A burning sensation triggered under her eyelids. What was supposed to be a joyous time of celebration was shifting into something that was bigger than her mind could fathom.

"Miss Meg, is everything okay?"

Startled by Corrine's presence, Meg yelled. "Oh, my God." She exhaled. "Corrine, I didn't realize you were in here," she explained.

"I was cleaning the mirrors in the bathroom." She gave Meg the once over as if uncertain of her strange behavior. Meg couldn't blame her. She was hiding after all — not exactly normal behavior for the owner of her own B&B."

Meg pointed back toward the door. "Right. I asked you to come up and make sure the empty rooms were tidy for our next round of guests. Silly me. I guess my mind was so preoccupied I had completely forgotten. Sorry about that, Corrine."

"Nervous about Ms. Emmerson's arrival, aren't you?"

Meg released her stiffened posture and walked toward Corrine. "Does it show?"

She loved Corrine from the moment they'd met. They clicked somewhat like kindred spirits, easily finishing the other's sentences, sharing common interests such as food, books, and their love for hospitality. Corrine was like the older, sweet aunt that Meg never had. For that matter, she didn't have any female influences after her mother died. At least not until Mariam came along. But, even that wasn't until many years into her adulthood.

"Nervous is an understatement."

Corrine laid her hand over Meg's. "Darlin', everything will be just fine. I've been reading up on Ms. Emmerson and the more I read the more I know her stay will be as easy as taking a walk in the park."

"What makes you say that?" Meg asked.

"Honey — my grandson bought me this little gadget right here —" she said, waving her tablet. "It has all you need to know from soup to nuts. At the touch of a few buttons I was able to pull up all of Ms. Emmerson's likes, dislikes and more. Oh, and I think it's safe to assume that she's coming here to get away from her lying, cheating, no good, scoundrel of a husband. Here's his picture right here — spotted in broad daylight with another woman."

Meg's eyes bulged. "Oh my. And, to think she'll be landing here on Harbour Island, staying at a B&B where the owners are getting married. Note to self... keep the wedding talk to a minimum. Got it."

The wedding talk wouldn't be the only thing they'd have to keep to keep at bay. If Meg's mental checklist was correct they were now balancing their ceremony, with the arrival of a high profile guest, and more importantly, her father who was potentially struggling with an addiction.

Chapter 5

Nora

"Where are you going?" The sound of Liam's voice startled Nora as she packed. She glared at him as he leaned in the entryway of her closet. His clothes were disheveled and his face was pale, looking like death warmed over— if there was such a thing.

She glanced at him, noticing he hadn't shaved, and his eyes looked bloodshot as if he hadn't slept. *Why would he lose sleep? Wasn't this the guy who was supposedly living his best life with his mistress — soon to be wife number two? Wasn't this the man who boldly announced his plans while standing outside his hotel room — the place where he performed all of his extra marital affairs? A guy like that couldn't possibly spend the night agonizing over anything or losing sleep —* she wondered.

"Where I'm going is none of your business. The only thing you need to be concerned with is where you're going because you sure as hell aren't staying here," she snarled, then reverted her attention back to her clothing.

With every drawer she sorted through, she wondered what

was brewing in his mind as he continued standing there, not saying a word.

Just as she reached for a hat the silence was broken. "Surely we're going to approach this in an amicable way. We have way too much history between us — and even if the marriage didn't work we've always been reasonable... sensible... there's no point in deviating from that now."

Nora stared at the floral jumpsuit hanging in her closet thinking it would be a perfect fit for an evening on Harbour Island. She also considered how delusional he must be if he thought she was about to be reasonable about anything.

"Ha." She chuckled. "Reasonable, he says. Please, Liam." She ran her hand across her bathing suits, choosing several to toss in her bag as she continued, "Sensible. Hmm. Would you like for me to be as reasonable and sensible as you were when you decided to have an affair?" she continued. "By the way. While we're on the topic, I've been meaning to ask you something."

He interrupted, "Nora, don't do this."

She darted her eyes across the closet, throwing a sharp dagger. "You don't get to cut me off, Liam. How long has this affair been going on?"

He hung his head and allowed his eyes to drift to the ground. "None of that matters anymore."

"It matters to me. I want to know how long you've been playing me for a fool and I'd much rather hear it from you than from social media."

He snapped. "You make it sound like this was done intentionally. I loved you, Nora. I — I still love you. But, you weren't available." He paused. "We weren't available for each other. And, I needed more."

She could hear the sound of him beginning to sob and turned to see him wiping his face. That's when it hit Nora that

Liam had been drinking. He didn't drink much, but when he did, he always became sappy and easily triggered.

"A man deserves to be —" He sniffled. "A man deserves —"

Sounding more abrupt than the first time she said, "If you think you're going to stand here and cry your way out of this, think again. All I want to know is how long."

His eyes met hers. Deep within, Nora wondered why she even cared to ask. Maybe it was the way her brain was wired as a journalist — always interested in investigating the next story line. Always interested in uncovering the truth, except this time she knew it would hurt.

"Two years," he admitted. He then wiped his mouth in a sloppy fashion. "Two years and now she wants nothing to do with me. According to her, this is all too messy. How did she say it?" he questioned. "Oh yeah, something about things getting way out of hand."

Nora watched as he slowly slid down the wall, landing on his bottom. *Was this his version of a pity party? Or a cry out for help?* she wondered.

"Let me get this straight. Your mistress. The woman I saw in the hotel — left you?"

He nodded in agreement. "Yep. She's gone. It's over. She wasn't too keen on our little conversation in the hallway. Especially the part where—" He stopped.

"What?"

He looked up. "Forget it. Like I said earlier. None of it matters."

Nora yanked several tops off the hangers in her closet and threw them into her luggage. She then reached for another pair of sandals before clearing an entire shelf of shoes onto the floor with one arm. "What a coward! What a coward you are to think that you can just walk all over me like this. Who was there for you when you were sick with death nearly staring you in the face? Me! Who helped you get back on your feet and supported all your career endeavors? Me. And, who stood by your side when no one else would — at times not even your own family? Me. And now, I ask you one simple question and you don't even have the decency to be straightforward with me. How dare you, Liam? How dare you!"

"Fine," he replied.

The surge of adrenaline running through her veins was enough to make her want to clear off another shelf, but instead Nora maintained her composure and listened.

"If you want to know, I'll tell you. But you're not going to like what I have to say."

The corner of her mouth curled upward.

"There were several women over the years, not just one," he admitted while continuing to hang his head low. "Chasing deals for the company on one hand and having women at my beck and call became like a sport. It was easy, a thrill, and a challenge all at the same time. And, sadly because of our lifestyles and the time spent apart..."

She interrupted, "Don't you dare. Don't blame this on anything other than yourself. Out of the two of us, I was just as busy, always slammed with work, but I was never disloyal to you, Liam. Never."

His brown eyes connected with hers in the most pathetic kind of way. "Well, then I'll take the blame. It was all me. I stepped outside the marriage and lived another life outside of this home. And —" The last words he uttered so quietly Nora squinted to ensure she was hearing him correctly. "In the midst of doing so, I fell in love."

Internally Nora heard a microphone drop to the floor. He'd said it. The dreaded words she was searching for which served as additional confirmation of his disloyalty. Not only had her husband stepped out on her to have an affair, but he actually loved the woman. She questioned why the hotel episode wasn't enough to cure her curiosity, but she was an investigator at heart, and now she had what she needed.

Chuckling in a not-so-friendly kind of way, Nora said, "Well, isn't that special. Tell me something, Liam. I'm just dying to know — if you two are so in love, why did she leave you? Why are you sitting in my closet looking like a lost puppy?"

He turned his cheek, facing in the other direction. "Last night she received a set of photos in the mail as well."

Nora immediately laughed it off. "What good would it do to send pictures of the two of you parading around Manhattan to her?" But no sooner than Nora vocalized the question did she realize what was really going on. Feeling stunned, she opened her mouth.

Liam began removing his loosely worn tie as he said, "Yeah well, the pictures were not of her and I. They were from a while back of me and another woman. A woman I'm no longer with. However, she doesn't believe me — and even if she did, there's apparently someone out there who's doing everything in their power to ruin my life. So — it's like I said. At this point, none of it matters. I just came in here to apologize to you — for the embarrassment and the shame. I'm almost certain the new photos will also start to surface. It's just a matter of time.

Nora froze, unable to breathe for what felt like a full minute. The saddest part was she knew Liam was only having this conversation with her because of the public repercussions. She didn't sense one ounce of true remorse or love for the woman he shared his last name with for twenty-five years. How a man could grow so cold was more than she'd ever understand.

Closing her eyes she asked, "Why Liam? Was it because I could never have your child?"

"No. That's so far behind us. You should leave it in the past where it belongs. You and I — we're just not compatible anymore. We're on two different paths now and we have been for a very long time. The best thing we can do at this point is let things die down publicly, end amicably, and go our separate —"

Nora held out her hand. "Please. Spare me with all the amicable talk. I haven't had much sleep, allowing me plenty of time to think things through. And, here's how I plan to move forward." She proceeded folding the remaining items for her bag. "I am leaving today for a nice, long, much needed vacation, at your expense. Upon my return, I expect to see that you and your belongings have been completely removed from this apartment."

Putting up opposition Liam argued, "And where am I supposed to live?"

Again Nora looked at him. This time with a blank stare as she tried to figure out who this man was standing in her closet. Outside of his physical appearance he was a complete stranger. The man she'd married over two decades ago was completely gone, replaced by an unrecognizable soul.

Calmly she replied, "I'm sure you'll figure something out."

Nora zipped up her bag and rolled past Liam. On the way out she shared one parting message. "In the spirit of being sensible, as you would say — if you lay a finger on the vacation properties, or other assets, I assure you by the time I'm done I'll take you for everything you're worth. Not because I need it, but because it's what you deserve."

Flight 827 to the Bahamas was smooth and brief, just the way Nora liked it. Her check-in at Seaside B&B also went smoothly with a friendly greeting from the staff and thankfully very little public attention.

In her room, she looked around at the freshly painted shiplap walls, seashell-shaped accent pillows, driftwood decor, and white chiffon curtains. She took it all in. But, as beautiful as it was, it was the sound of the ocean that drew her in the most.

Nora slid open the glass door, took in a deep breath and exhaled a heart-wrenching cry. Internally she vowed to press forward onto the next chapter of her life. But not before releasing one last cry to shed the heartache and shame.

* * *

Nora Emmerson let off her pillow, startled by the sound of someone knocking at her door. For a moment, she'd lost all track of time as she drifted off into a sound sleep. Outside the sun was setting and her phone was buzzing with ten missed messages.

"Who is it?" she called.

"It's your hostess, Meg. We met when you arrived. I'm here to deliver the meal you requested at seven. I can come back if you'd prefer."

She smoothed over her clothing while easing out of bed. "No, you're fine. I'll be right there."

Noticing her assistant Camille had been the one eagerly texting, she messaged back that all was well and laid the phone down.

At the door, Nora put on her best smile and welcomed Meg to come in.

"You'll have to forgive my appearance. I guess I dozed off and lost track of time."

Meg smiled, laying down her tray. "It's the sound of the ocean. It will do it to you every single time. Besides, we're here to serve you. If extra rest is what you need we can always adjust the schedule, no worries."

"Thank you," Nora replied.

Meg pointed to the tray. "As requested our chef put together conch tacos with a house salad and a soda. Chef Sean is known for adding his signature flavors to all of his meals and takes great pride in it. If there's anything else that you need just ring the front desk and we'll be happy to serve."

Nora smiled but could feel her swollen eyelids as Meg spoke to her. She knew it wouldn't last forever — the crying, and recalling conversations with Liam line by line, while trying to make sense of it all. This is not how she was planning to celebrate fifty years of life. And, with her birthday weekend coming up, she'd have to find a way to jumpstart the new year on a positive note, which means she had a lot of work to do.

"Meg, thank you. This all looks wonderful. But, if you wouldn't mind, I'd like to have a little heart-to-heart," Nora explained.

"Sure."

Nora inhaled then said, "I'm assuming either you or your staff members heard about —"

Not being able to finish her sentence, she paused.

"I don't know much." Meg gently waved, dismissing the idea. "You can't believe what you hear in the tabloids. And, the good news is we're not focused on that kind of stuff here on Harbour Island. Harbour is a small little island with pink sands, relaxing ocean vibes, and with friendly people who live free from the hustle and bustle of the mainland."

Nora relaxed her shoulders. "Thank you for that. I'm not sure what my assistant requested, but I just wanted to offer that you and your staff don't have to worry about having a high maintenance celebrity around. While I'm out here, I have a lot of soul searching to do, but I'm also taking off my celebrity hat.

It's nothing but a ridiculous status that we as humans give ourselves when we think we've achieved some level of public fame. Big whoop. From this point on, I'm no longer Ms. Emmerson to you or anyone else who works here. You can refer to me by my maiden name, Nora Hutchins. Better yet, Nora will suffice," she said, extending her hand.

"Ok, Nora. Well, as I would tell any guest, it's a pleasure to have you with us," Meg said, shaking her hand in return.

"Yes, and during your wedding week. I should say the pleasure is all mine. It feels good to know I'm keeping company with people who are happy, in love, and soon to be married."

Meg's eyes widened. "How did you know?"

Nora chuckled. "Research is what I do for a living. That plus your wedding announcement was posted in the Caribbean Journal."

Meg nodded. "Ah, yes. How could I forget? Well, I can assure you that when myself and Parker are not here, Corinne and Chef Sean will continue to take excellent care. All you have to do is ring the —"

"The front desk, I know. And, I thank you in advance for that. I'll certainly use your services when needed, but a part of my time spent here is going to be getting out, and living, and having new experiences. I'm celebrating my fiftieth this week and I want it to be memorable. At minimum — I don't want it to include memories from this past week, that's for sure."

Watching Meg's face light up helped put Nora at ease. There was something about her presence and the B&B that was warm and welcoming, making her feel right at home. Better yet, even better than being at home — which was just what she needed during her time away.

"Nora, I'd be happy to make some recommendations. If you like listening to good music or participating in Karaoke, there's Daddy D's or Beyond the Reef. And, if the nightlife isn't your cup of tea, then there's always water sports like kayaking and deep-sea diving."

She laughed. "How about some good old-fashioned sunbathing to begin with? Then we can take it from there."

"Of course we can start with sunbathing." Meg leaned in, lowering her voice. "If I'm not overstepping my boundaries, I know it may not seem like it right now, but, the pain won't last forever. You're going to wake up one day and realize there are bigger and better plans in store for you. A better life awaits you."

Nora sighed. "Really? I'm glad you're so confident because as you said, it sure doesn't feel like it."

"Trust me, I've been where you are. Our stories may have their own different twists, but the overall idea is the same. I was supposed to be married to some self-proclaimed big shot who's family came from wealth. We were supposed to live our fairy-tale lives in Manhattan together where we would have it all. Unfortunately, he struggled with infidelity," Meg explained.

"Hmm, that's putting it mildly. I call it having a hard time keeping one's pants zipped up," Nora said, putting it bluntly.

"You have a point there. Either way, that was the worst and best time of my life all wrapped up in one. The worst because of the hurt and deceit. The best because he paved the way for me to meet the love of my life," Meg replied.

"Hmm."

Over her years in journalism Nora had heard of many stories filled with second chances. A second chance at life after a near death experience was one of the more popular stories. But love? After dedicating so many years to the same person who would in the end betray her? She wasn't so sure her heart would ever recover. Would she move on and enjoy her life — yes. But, recover enough to love again? That was a tough one.

Meg continued, "Look. If you want to be surrounded by

women who know all about moving on after experiencing extreme heartache, my friend Frankie and I will be around. Well, perhaps you can talk to her after she gets over being such a super fan. But, seriously speaking, we've been through the fire, and we're still here. Even Parker and I — we were able to beat unbelievable odds. So, just know you're not alone."

Nora placed her hands in a position of prayer. "Thank you, Meg."

"You're welcome. Now please, go ahead and eat your conch tacos while it's still hot. Chef Sean will never let me hear the end of it if you have it any other way."

Chapter 6

Meg

Meg pushed open the front door of the house at 3011 Seaside Drive. A lot of progress had been made with renovations to their newest edition, and within just a few short weeks they'd host their first wedding for Frankie and David. Afterward, they'd officially open their second B&B to the public. For Parker and Meg, it was an exciting undertaking as they had already secured reservations for their first guest.

"So, what do you think, Dad?" she asked.

Sam gazed around the entryway, seemingly amazed at the grand windows with a seaside view. "I'm speechless. This place is gorgeous, honey. It looks nothing like you originally described."

Meg smiled. "That's a good thing. There was so much dust and old wallpaper everywhere I was having a hard time seeing Parker's vision. But, somehow him, his sister Savannah, and Miguel, they all managed to pull it together. Now, all that's left to do is splash a little paint in the gift shop, and we'll be up and running full steam ahead."

She led him down the main hall showing him the grand living room. It was the perfect place for guests to gather for evening cocktails, mingle, or simply relax if they chose to do so.

Sam ran his hand along a chaise lounge. "A beachfront property like this could easily come with a price tag in the millions. You two certainly got yourselves the deal of a lifetime, working with Old Man Barnes. It's sad he still isn't here to see how lovely things turned out."

Meg rested in one of the chairs, motioning for her father to join her. "I couldn't agree more, but he was sick, Dad. If being here meant he'd have to continue to suffer then I'm glad he's finally at peace."

Her father nodded. "True indeed."

She contemplated whether to ask him the question that had been reeling in the back of her mind. Being honest with herself, there was no way Meg would make it through the rest of the week's festivities without knowing what was going on with her father.

She cleared her throat and said, "To me, one of the saddest parts about Barnes' untimely passing was his relationship with his estranged son, Devon. I think if they'd had the chance to talk there would've been so much that Barnes would want to say. There were so many things he wanted to share with his son if only he had the chance."

"That is sad, dear. That's why it's important to stay as closely connected with your loved ones as possible. However small our family is I'd like to think we're all close and there for one another. That's what matters most."

Meg thought about it, agreeing for the most part. They were close, but clearly not enough that he would open up and share his struggles with the ones he loved and trusted. The question was — why was he holding back? What was going on in his life that was so bad that it was worthy of hiding from the rest of the family?

"Dad—"

Still looking upward at the beams he replied, "Yes, dear? Sorry, I'm just captivated by all the gorgeous and meticulous work done by your soon to be husband. I have to bring Mariam over here before the week is over so she can see it for herself. My description wouldn't do the place any justice."

Meg looked upward as well. "You should. But, while I have you here there's something I've been meaning to ask you."

"Sure, honey. What is it?"

As Meg locked eyes with her father the doorbell rang, followed by a grand entrance from Parker, followed by Meg's childhood friend, Casey.

"Hey, how come no one told us there was a gathering happening over at 3011? I would've brought over a bottle of champagne," Parker announced.

Meg leapt up reaching toward her friend, embracing her with a long hug. "Oh, my goodness. Look at you, Case. You look so amazing," she squealed.

"Mm, if only you knew. I had to search the racks high and low to find the perfect sundress to help hide all the extra weight that I've gained. Thanks for the compliment just the same." She drew back, looking at Meg. "You, on the other hand, are glowing." Giving Parker a nudge on the arm, she said, "You must be taking good care of my girl. She looks fantastic."

Unable to contain her joy, Meg nearly forgot about her pending chat with her dad. Other than showing him the place, it was the main reason she took time to steal away and be alone with him. Clearly now, the conversation would have to wait.

"I'm doing everything I can to make sure Meg has the life that she deserves," Parker replied. "As for her good looks, that comes naturally. Isn't that right, Sam?"

Sam chuckled, pointing toward Parker. "You're my kind of guy, Parker. You know exactly what to say to keep a woman happy. Take it from me, that kind of attitude will go a long way in your marriage, Son. A very long way."

Meg joined in on the fun. "Are you teaching him how to butter me up? That's terrible advice."

They all laughed.

She continued, "Come on everybody. Let's get back to the main house. I can't wait to spend some time catching up with my god children."

* * *

Later on, when everyone went their separate way, settling in for the evening Meg lingered at the B&B with Parker.

She picked up a pencil, making a list of last minute items needed for the rehearsal dinnerwhile he massaged her shoulders.

"I don't know about you, but I think this week is getting off to a pretty decent start, don't you think?" he asked.

"It's a busy start for sure."

Parker kissed her on the neck. "Yes, busy, but in a good way. Your parents are here, my parents will be arriving soon. Oh, and let's not forget Ms. Emmerson who's been an absolute low-maintenance dream. She's so preoccupied, it's like she's not even here," he said.

"Mm-hmm. By the way, she'd prefer to go by Nora Hutchins. Nora, to be exact. Have you checked in with Corinne to make sure she has everything covered?"

Meg could feel his hands kneading in deeper, making it difficult to concentrate.

"I did and all is well. The only thing I want you to be concerned about is enjoying this week. I don't want our wedding day to fly by without us enjoying it and taking it all in."

Meg looked around. "Agreed. But we did set ourselves up with a bit of a chaotic schedule. All things considered; I still think we're doing a good job. We have it under control."

She slid her hands along his chest and closed her eyes. "Just think. In a few short days it will be official. We'll be husband and wife — till death do us part."

Parker slipped his lips over her ear lobe. "Forever and ever — Amen." He lowered his voice to a whisper. "I don't know if I've ever told you this, Meg. There's not a day that goes by where I don't long to be with you. You are my lover and my best friend, and I can't wait to make this official." He kissed her again, then said, "I just have so much peace about everything. Don't you?"

Peace was the last word that came to mind when it came to her dad. And while this was her wedding week — and she knew the only thing she should be focused on was marrying Parker, she just couldn't shake the thoughts stirring around in her head. She couldn't stop mentally replaying the conversation she'd overheard.

Meg sighed. "About us, yes. I have all the peace in the world. But —"

"Uh-oh. What is it?" he asked, slumping down on the couch next to her.

Meg nodded and returned to her list. "Nevermind. It's probably nothing."

"You can't nevermind me after I pour out my heart like that. Tell me — what's bothering you?"

She laid her pencil in the crease of her notebook and closed it.

"It's my dad. He hasn't been acting like himself ever since they arrived. He's either overly tired or frustrated or —"

Parker placed his hand over hers. "You might want to cut him some slack. He has much more of a laid back kind of schedule now that he's retired. At least that's the way he describes it. But, this week has been anything but laid back from the time they arrived. He probably just needs some rest."

Meg nodded. "No, I think there's more to it than that."

She could feel Parker's eyes as he watched her, waiting for some sort of clarity.

"Promise you won't say anything?" Meg asked.

"Oh, dear. Why am I getting a funny feeling about whatever you're about to say?"

She nudged him. "Parker, stop. This is serious."

He rolled his eyes. "Okay, I'm listening."

Wishing she could make more sense of what she overheard, Meg repositioned herself to face Parker and explain. "I think my dad is battling with some kind of addiction. I just can't put my finger on the details. I was tidying up in one of the suites yesterday, when I overheard him and Mariam arguing. They kept referring to his sleeping pills, and describing behavior that was out of character for my dad. Mariam was insistent that he needs to see their doctor back home. I'm really worried, Parker."

His eyebrows folded. "Oh, wow, I'm sorry. I had no idea."

"That's just it. I had no idea either. And, if it weren't for me passing by their room, I still wouldn't have known. Ever since I moved out here I feel like the step-child that's always the last to find things out. Important things, no less," she confessed.

Meg sat there, watching as Parker turned away, seemingly digesting everything she was saying. So, she continued explaining, "I started to bring it up when I was giving him the tour of 3011, but we were interrupted. Now, I'm second guessing everything. What do you think I should do?"

"If you ask me, you can do whatever you want, but saying

something will probably make a bad situation worse," he replied.

Meg frowned. "How so? I could potentially help my father get back on track. Who knows? Maybe there's a deeper rooted issue behind all this and if he sits down and talks to someone it could make all the difference."

"Meg, not only does your father have a wife who loves and cares for him, but you also said she mentioned seeing a doctor. For now, that should be enough for you. I would stay out of it and allow your father time to come and talk to you when he's ready."

In that moment, Meg didn't know what was agitating her more — the fact that what Parker was suggesting wasn't wrong, but it just wasn't what she wanted to hear, or the fact that he may have been right — but she just wanted him to be supportive and agree with her.

She continued, "Think about it. Maybe the fact that I over-heard them, when I ordinarily wouldn't be able to, was a sign so that I could help."

Again, Parker reached over, this time touching her shoul-der. "Babe, don't take this the wrong way. But the last time you overheard something, you only heard part of the story, taking the rest out of context and it nearly cost us our relationship. This time, I'd like to think you're looking for a different kind of outcome."

Meg glanced at Parker thinking that somehow all the things she usually admired about him and even found attractive were the very things plucking her nerves in that moment. All she wanted was his support. And all she wanted was to help her dad.

"Wow, you just said a mouthful. Not only are you implying that I was at fault for nearly ending our relationship, when in fact you were the one going through some sort of midlife crisis—"

"Meg," he pleaded.

"Oh no, please allow me to finish. You're also implying that I'm poking my nose around in my dad's business when all I'm trying to do is help him. How could you go there, Parker? You know my dad has had health issues in the past, and all I want is what's best for him."

"Sweetheart, all I'm trying to suggest is that you go about this differently. Allowing him time to sort through this and come to you when he's ready is not the end of the world. In doing so, you're showing him that you respect and trust his process, instead of doing it the other way around," he explained.

"So — if I had brought it up with him this evening, I would've been demonstrating disrespect and distrust?"

Parker got up from the couch and made his way halfway across the room before turning around to make his point. "Look, I don't want to argue with you, Meg. All I was trying to suggest is your father deserves the option of coming to talk to you when he's ready, instead of being shocked to know you were eavesdropping when he thought he was having a private conversation with Mariam."

As he spoke, Meg's eyes shifted in slow motion toward her father entering the room. That's when her mouth dropped out of sheer embarrassment. If Parker's biggest concern was about Meg revealing how much she knew, it wouldn't matter now.

Samuel had walked in and overheard everything, leaving a lot for them to explain.

* * *

"May I ask what this is about?" Samuel uttered.

Bouncing to her feet, Meg replied, "Dad, I thought you were settled in for the evening. Is everything okay?"

He glanced at Parker and then back to Meg while slipping his hands in his pockets. "Well, I don't know. I was hoping you'd tell me since I appear to be the topic of conversation. What exactly did you overhear that has you so up in arms?

If there were ever a moment where Meg felt like she could be sick to her stomach, it was now. Yes, she wanted to talk to her father. But, not like this. "I —"

Parker jumped in, "Sam, Meg was just telling me how—"

Sam interrupted, "It's okay, Parker. It's noble of you to try and step in, but if Meg was eavesdropping, I'd like to know what she heard. Meg, please explain."

All Meg was trying to do was the right thing, yet it felt like the wrong thing as she stood there with sweaty palms, nervous like a child. Perhaps Parker was right. Maybe it wasn't worth it. Unfortunately, it was too late now.

"I overheard you and Mariam arguing about the pills, and you having difficulty with sleep. And — I just want to offer my support in whatever way I can. If seeing the doctor in New York is what you need, Dad, then maybe listening to Mariam is the best thing." She paused. "Sleeping pills can be really addicting, and sometimes we think we're in control of things, but we're really not."

On the sidelines she saw Parker backing off a bit.

Samuel continued. "Is that all?"

"Well — yes, but. I was hoping we could sit down and talk about it. I mean, are you struggling with sleep apnea, or perhaps something else? Whatever it is, we can help you get to the bottom of it, Dad. As a family — there's nothing we can't overcome."

A stern expression washed over his face, causing him to turn beat red. "Again, are you finished?"

"Yes," Meg responded with a voice that was practically at a low whisper.

"Good, because if I needed help, I would've asked for it. I'm completely fine and as far as I'm concerned Mariam is overexaggerating the matter. Not that I should have to explain that to anybody. Next time, I'd suggest you take Parker's advice. A grown woman eavesdropping at her father's door is beneath you, Meg. Please — respect my privacy."

Meg stared at the door practically feeling a cold breeze as she watched her father exit the room. The stern demeanor he displayed wasn't like him, making it even more obvious that something was truly wrong.

Parker cried out, "Meg, I'm sorry. I didn't realize he was standing there."

Unfortunately, aggravation stewed on the inside, causing Meg to remain silent, throw a dagger toward Parker, then exit the room.

Chapter 7

Nora

"Thank you, Camille. I owe you big time." Nora smiled as she buried her feet deeper into the sand.

Fighting off phone calls from studio executives who were now beginning to worry had become a full time task for her assistant, Camille. Unfortunately, Nora wasn't ready to face them yet, so if setting her phone to voicemail was what she had to do then so be it.

Most mornings she wasn't even ready to face herself or her present reality, let alone people who'd actually want explanations and answers.

This morning's revelation as she lied in bed had been so eye-opening. Most people she knew had a midlife crisis simply because they weren't ready to embrace becoming older. Those types of meltdowns resulted in big purchases of sports cars, private jets, or something fun and exhilarating.

She on the other hand was experiencing a midlife crisis due to her husband's careless affair. And, to make matters worse, the jerk wasn't even sorry.

"No problem, boss. I explained that you needed time to clear your head. Let's face it, this whole ordeal has been very traumatic. I encouraged them to see it as a time for you to hit the reset button, so you could come back refreshed and reenergized."

"Hmm," Nora replied.

"Wrong choice of words?"

"Not really. That is the whole point of this trip. Sadly, I'm having a hard time getting my mind to follow suit. All I can seem to envision is the sloppy look on Liam's face as he admitted that he was in love," she replied with disdain.

"What?"

"Nevermind. Forget I ever uttered the words. Reliving that whole experience over and over defeats the whole purpose of me coming here," Nora said.

"True. Well, how are you enjoying the B&B so far?"

Nora lowered her lounge chair and slid her beach hat over her eyes. "It's perfect. Kudos to you and your friends for the recommendation. So far everyone has been very accommodating, yet giving me the space that I need. The grounds are filled with gorgeous flowers and beautiful views of the ocean. It's all I could've ever asked for. Certainly way better than staying at a crowded hotel."

Camille perked up. "That sounds nice. Now, if we could just get you out and about — maybe even meet a companion to help take your mind off things. That might not be a bad idea, you know."

"Camille, the last thing I need is to meet someone else who will be just as careless with my heart as Liam was. No, thank you. There will be no dating for me. That ship has sailed."

"I understand. No one is trying to suggest that you start dating so soon. I just said, be open to meeting a companion.

Someone to talk to on the trip. You know — to help take your mind off things. That's all."

"Mmm. And, who are you supposed to be, my therapist?" she teased.

"Nora, just trust me, please. I haven't failed you yet, have I?"

"No."

"Good. Now go meet people and have fun. Next time we speak I want a full report, including the name of at least one guy you made small talk with," Camille replied.

"But."

"No buts. It's all a part of your journey to healing. Now get out there and mingle. Maybe even flirt a little. I gotta run. Talk to you soon. Bye."

Nora held her cell phone up, looking at the screen which had returned to normal. Camille had to be out of her sweet mind if she thought Nora was capable of doing such a thing. She'd conquer this eventually, but right now it hurt too much, feeling like a fresh sting that wouldn't go away.

* * *

* * *

Spending hours being kissed by the sun had left Nora feeling drained and ready to head inside. She wrapped herself in a sheer coverup, slipping on her shades and mysterious beach hat as not to be discovered. Although, truth be told, the island vibe was so peaceful it didn't seem to matter. Seaside B&B was the one place she felt like she could be herself without anybody really caring.

Looking downward as she gracefully treaded through the sand, she bumped into a tall man.

Nora stepped to the left, and so did he. She then stepped to the right, and he did as well. That's when they both realized their little dance was getting them nowhere.

He spoke first, "Pardon me. I wasn't watching where I was going."

The deep voice attached to the hairy-chested male figure captured her attention.

"Uh, It was probably my fault. I guess my mind was elsewhere and I —"

Her eyes roamed from his lips, to his beard, down his masculine chest and then she caught herself. "It was probably me. Sitting out in the sun makes me feel loopy. As in drained, tired. Sleepy, is what I meant to say. Yep, sleepy."

Nora, go inside before you start babbling like an idiot, she thought.

He smiled. "Understood. I'm heading inside as well. Just came back to grab my sunglasses. Didn't realize I'd left them behind until I stepped inside the B&B."

She paused, taking in every muscle, his glistening skin, and the friendliness of his smile. "Do you mean, Seaside B&B?"

He turned slightly, pointing in that direction. "Yeah, are you staying there as well? I know the owners."

Secretly hoping she'd make the way she was scoping his body behind her sunglasses she replied, "Oh, that's wonderful. Yes, I'm staying there as well and so far it's been beautiful. They seem like such a sweet couple." She then looked around as not to be so obvious. "Plus, the service has been impeccable. It's my understanding they're getting married this weekend."

He smiled even harder while raising a finger. "That's why I'm here actually. I'm friends with Parker. I'm actually responsible for helping him take over the ownership here at the B&B." He extended his hand. "The name is Chuck. Chuck Nesbit."

Nora slipped her hand into his. "Mr. Nesbit, it's nice to meet you."

"Please, call me Chuck."

"Okay, Chuck. So, you're the one behind the making of this beautiful establishment?"

He laughed. "Well, not quite the making of it, but certainly I was the one responsible for telling Parker about this amazing deal. I work in real estate, specializing in bank owned properties. I actually used to live in the area and had the privilege of introducing Parker to the man who sold him the B&B."

She noticed him stopping to admire her. "There's actually a lot of history behind this place. It's a pretty neat story if you have time to hear it on the way back up."

Nora's instincts kicked in, realizing she'd probably be better off continuing her solo journey to her room. "That's kind of you, but I don't want to keep you. Besides, I ordered a meal to be delivered to my room in about —" She glanced at the time on her phone. "Ooh, precisely ten minutes."

"Alright. Certainly, I don't want to get in the way of a hungry woman." Again he smiled, then shifted to the side.

"Although, I don't think I got your name," he added.

Hearing the sound of Camille's voice egging her on in her head, she said. "Nora."

"Beautiful name. It was nice meeting you."

She waved. "Take care."

On the walk back to the B&B, Nora thought long and hard about the road ahead. She'd been out of the dating game for so long, never once considering anyone else while she was married. That's why today's brief encounter was rather telling. If making small talk with a gorgeous man was going to turn Nora into a rambling idiot, perhaps she needed to pass on that too.

* * *

"Room service," a female voice called.

Nora clipped her hair back and headed for the door. Being greeted by a warm smile from the staff was all she needed to put her mind at ease.

As she opened the door wider, a sweet woman smiled. "Ms. Nora, I am Corrine from guest services and housekeeping. I will be serving you this evening. How do you do?"

"It's nice to meet you, Corrine. I'm well, thank you," Nora replied.

"The pleasure is all mine. It's my understanding that you requested the conch tacos again." Corrine leaned in, whispering. "It's actually one of Chef Sean's favorite meals to cook."

"Well, please relay the message to Chef Sean that he's doing an amazing job with the dish. This is only my second night but I'm absolutely hooked. I can't seem to get enough of it."

"I'll be sure to let him know. In the meantime, I'm happy to leave your food wherever you'd like, but can I make a suggestion?" Corrine asked.

"Sure."

As Nora motioned for Corrine to come in she listened very intently, observing that she was a mature woman with a sweet demeanor, and looked as if she possessed the wisdom of a ninety-year-old. Corrine was definitely the kind of woman anyone could feel comfortable talking to.

She stopped the cart and pointed toward the window. "Do you see that wonderful view?"

Nora smiled. "How could I miss it? It's the most attractive feature of the room."

"Right. Outside there's a beautiful island that awaits you. Again, I'm happy to serve you wherever you'd like, but are you aware that we have a guest area downstairs where you can take in more ocean views while enjoying the company of others? No one is going to bother you out here. Trust me, the only thing people are after is tranquility."

Corrine closed her eyes for a moment, breathing in the evening breeze. "It feels good, doesn't it?" She smiled.

Nora walked over to the window. "It sure does. I guess that's the trade winds kicking in. Or maybe even an incoming storm. Either way it feels heavenly."

"My point exactly. Why would anyone want to keep themselves all cooped up inside of a room, knowing they could explore and perhaps experience a slice of heaven?" Corrine urged.

Nora's eyes fell downward out of embarrassment. She admittedly was hiding from the rest of the world. For her, hiding had been much easier than facing her truth.

Corrine slipped her a business card. "Now, there's a brave soul downstairs who asked me to pass this along to you. He's a friend of the owners, safe, nice guy, and apparently would love to meet you for dessert in an hour. If you're interested, here's his number. If not — he's a big boy, and can handle the rejection," she teased. She then placed the card in Nora's hand. "In the meantime, don't hesitate to call if you need me. I'll be right downstairs."

Nora held the card up. "Thank you."

Corrine smiled again and then closed the door behind her.

* * *

For the last forty-five minutes Nora unapologetically sunk her teeth into her conch tacos, watched the sun shift over the ocean, and occasionally read the headlines on the big screen of the local news.

There wasn't one ounce of her that missed being in the spotlight, broadcasting from the big desk, or even being a public figure. Instead she was enjoying her newfound version of peace.

No sooner than the thought hit her did she take her last sip of her drink and glanced at the business card. "Chuck Nesbit. Specializing in Bank Owned Properties. Interesting," she read aloud.

Sliding the card closer to her she thought, *So, you want to meet for dessert, Mr. Nesbit.*

She sat contemplating what may have triggered the invite. Was it her celebrity status? What else could it be? That was one of the problems with being single and having to start over again. Every man would always want a piece of her fame and her bank account. There was no avoiding it. As a result, she didn't know if she'd ever remarry again.

Of course you want to meet for dessert. Men love dessert. It's what they live for, she thought.

On the flipside, she forced herself to consider Corrine's words which had to carry some weight. He was friends with the owners who seemed sweet enough. And, he said he was attending their wedding. That had to count for something, right?

Was she being a prude by staying to herself in the room, and occasionally laying by herself on the beach? This trip was supposed to be about her renewal and her healing. But, who said that healing had to take place all alone?

You're kidding yourself if you think you're going to go downstairs and make nice with a guy you barely know. It's too soon. Plus, you're not even divorced yet, she continued thinking as she cleared the table and removed her trash.

Then Nora stopped in front of the mirror. Letting her hair down, she tilted her head to the side, observing herself, starting with the signs of her first tan line, her shapely hips, and even her hair that was still wavy from being wet, yet beautiful.

Why me? she whispered, nearly shedding a tear.

Easing away from the mirror, Nora knew what she had to offer on the inside was far greater than what she saw externally. If Liam didn't get that, it was his loss. Not hers.

She then glanced at the card one more time and reached for her phone.

* * *

Just looking at the fine specimen of a man walking toward her was enough to trigger her heartbeat into an unusual pattern. Was Chuck this good looking when she ran into him earlier? Or was her second tropical beverage kicking in? For a non-drinker, it could've been a little of both. After sitting at the bar thinking it over for twenty minutes, her newfound commitment to get out and live a little gave her the green light to explore.

As he walked toward her she said, "Chuck. Nora Hutchins, nice to see you again." She smiled, extending her hand in a nervous, and business-like manner.

He gently took her by the hand. "Ah, this time I get a first and last name. We're making it," he said, then kissed her hand. "The pleasure is all mine. Thank you for joining me. For a minute there, I didn't think you'd respond."

Feeling a little silly, she replied, "Well, if I'm being honest I almost didn't, but they say the only real way to beat this thing is to get out there and have a good time, so —"

Looking confused, he replied, "I'm sorry?"

Nora glanced at him, stopping nothing short at noticing how well put together he looked.

She laughed. "You don't have to pretend like you don't

know. It's okay. The whole world practically knows what I'm talking about at this point," she explained, waving it off.

Noticing him draw his eyebrows together made the conversation feel even more awkward.

Surely he knew who she was? Didn't he?

She continued, "Sooo, how about that sunset? Stunning, isn't it?"

"I can think of something that's even more stunning," he responded. And, although it sounded cheesy, he looked sincere.

With her adrenaline pumping at full speed, she began fanning herself. "Look. That's sweet of you and all but, I probably should warn you in advance."

She felt so un-lady like considering all the thoughts that were running through her head. Was this even normal? Here she was at fifty-years old, lost and still trying to figure out what to do with her newfound freedom.

"Warn me?" He chuckled. "That's never a good sign on a first date."

Nora's eyes widened. "Date? Oh, no. This is not a date. I just came down to meet over a light dessert. I figured maybe I could hear the story about how the B&B came about and all but — a date?"

Chuck raised both hands simultaneously. "I'm sorry. Maybe that wasn't the right choice of words. In my mind, I'm in town for the weekend for my friend's wedding and as luck would have it, I return to the beach to get my sunglasses and come across this gorgeous woman, and I don't know. Something came over me, so I thought I would take a chance and invite her out. If the idea of this being a date is too forward, my apologies. I understand."

Just looking at him and seeing how crushed he was over the idea was enough to make her even more curious.

"Sooo — you really don't know who I am?" she asked.

He looked over his shoulder, to one side and then the other. "I'm sorry, but should I?"

That's when it hit her. It was just as Meg had said. The people out here didn't care about her status. Perhaps she'd been taking herself way too seriously.

She smiled. "Nevermind, it's probably the beverage talking. I probably need to quit while I'm ahead." She shoved her glass back across the counter. "How about we grab a table and see what Chef Sean has on the dessert menu?"

With one swift movement, she stood up and stumbled forward into his arms. Staring straight into his hazel eyes lasted for what felt like a full minute before Nora regained clarity of mind. "I promise it's not the alcohol. I usually don't even drink."

The warmth of his breath, coupled with his arms holding hers was enough to send chills up her spine.

He laughed, then looked downward. "I believe you. As a matter of fact, I think your broken heel might have something to do with it."

Feeling like a complete idiot, Nora pulled away slowly and looked down at her shoe.

"Go figure." She grunted.

Nora imagined what it would've been like to fall into his arms for something other than her dumb heel. If she could feel his sultry lips — just one time. Oh, what a nice distraction it would be.

"I'm sorry. Clearly, I'm incapable of holding myself together this evening." She picked up the heel while shifting a time or two to keep steady. "Actually, I'm not surprised. This is what I get for trying to fit in with the rest of society and act normal."

"Come again?" he replied.

Nora took one brief look into his eyes, then let the verbal

flood gates loose. She didn't cry or anything, but she could no longer hold back about her current emotional state of mind.

"Not exactly the kind of thing one brings up over dessert but — " She looked down at her shoe. "Since the evening is already going horribly wrong, I may as well come out with it. I'm in the process of getting a divorce. There. The cat's out of the bag."

"Oh."

She nodded. "Yep. Annnd, while I'd like to forget about all of it completely, every now and again something happens that brings the son of a gun to my remembrance."

"I see," he replied.

She held up the heel. "These dumb shoes were supposed to be an apology gift for an evening where he left me sitting alone at dinner. He'd completely forgotten about me, just as he'd done several times before. He was probably with one of his —" She paused, realizing she'd probably already scared him enough. "Anyway, it only makes sense that the heel would break on me when all I'm trying to do is move on and live my life. What do they call that, again? Karma?"

Nora flopped down on the chair in absolute shame. She knew nothing about how to carry herself on a non-date, or even how to have a basic conversation with an attractive gentleman. And, according to her self-pity, she'd obviously learned nothing about how to be a good wife. Therefore, the only thing she felt good at was being a professional workaholic.

Chuck bent down slightly, aligning his eyes with hers. "Could you wait right here for a second? I'll be right back. Ok?"

"Where are you going?"

She watched as he held his hands out. "Trust me. You won't move, will you?"

Nora glanced at her feet and then back at him. "Even if I tried, I wouldn't make it very far." She smiled.

"Good. I'll be right back."

She didn't know where the scrumptious hunk of a man was going, but if he'd managed to survive listening to her emotional tantrum, and it still didn't scare him away — the least she could do is wait for him.

Chapter 8

Meg

"To be honest, I'm starting to think having the wedding this weekend was a terrible idea," Meg said as she paced in front of her girlfriends, Casey and Frankie.

A walking excursion around the grounds of the B&B with her best friends was supposed to be calming, but instead Meg was starting to feel worse.

"Meg, what would make you say such a thing? What's going on?" Casey said.

"Is it the stress?" Frankie asked.

"No. Well, sort of. But, not really."

Allowing her hair to blow in the wind while taking a deep breath still didn't suppress her anguish.

"I'm so angry with Parker, I don't know what to do," Meg confessed.

"Parker? Why? Things were fine the last time I was here. I mean, I know you were trying to figure out the whole balancing act between the wedding and Nora Emmerson's arrival but —"

Casey interrupted, "Wait a minute. The Nora Emmerson is staying at Seaside B&B? As in, the anchor Nora Emmerson?"

Meg nodded. "Yes."

"As in, she's sleeping in the same dwelling where I'm currently staying?" Casey continued pressing.

Meg looked her in the eye. "Yes. And should either one of you run into her, please treat her like you would any other guest. Which really means — don't make her feel like she's different. She's already going through a lot right now. We promised her a relaxing experience and I want to see to it that she has one."

Frankie saluted. "Aye-aye, captain. We know the drill and will be happy to comply. Besides, after reading the headlines, I can see why she needed time away. It wouldn't be me, though. If I were in her shoes I'd be back in New York dragging his name through the mud, then sock him with a court date and alimony. I'd teach him to never embarrass me publicly or privately again. However, I digress. This isn't about Nora. This is about you."

Casey agreed, "Yes, tell us what happened."

Meg exhaled. "It seems like ever since my father and Mariam arrived it's been one thing or another. This week was supposed to be a happy time, but dad is battling with something and he's been trying to hide it. It's altering his mood and everything about him just seems off. And, I get that he's trying to suppress what he's going through, just so everyone else can be happy this week. But, you guys know me. I'd rather just know what's going on and deal with it. Plus, he needs to stop trying to be superman all the time. He can't handle everything on his own."

"Okayyy." Casey listened.

She continued, "Then there's Parker. When I confided in him about an argument I overheard between dad and Mariam, he took my father's side and made me look foolish in front of him," Meg explained, then dabbed her eyes. "The only thing I needed from him was his support, but instead he found a way to help make matters worse."

Frankie blurted out, "That doesn't sound like something Parker would do. You sure there wasn't just a misunderstanding?"

Meg retorted, "Trust me. He was taking my father's side, managing to say all the wrong things just as my father walked into the room and overheard us. He basically accused me of interfering in so many words — which gave my father the green light to agree and storm out of the room."

"Oh, no. I'm sorry, Meg," Casey said, rubbing her back. "But, you have to know this will blow over soon. You and Parker mean the world to each other."

Meg stopped in her tracks. "Yeah, but one would think he would've just been there for me. At that very moment when I confided in him was not the time for him to try and prove a point." She continued walking. "He even went as far as suggesting that my snooping could be troublesome. He said it nearly cost us our relationship in the past. How dare he paint me in such a negative light? Should I have been listening in? No. But they were loud enough that what was being said couldn't be missed — and if I'm able to help my father as a result then why should it matter? He's getting older now. It's not like I'll have him around forever."

In a calming voice, Casey replied, "I understand, but getting so upset within days of your wedding isn't going to help the situation.

Meg continued pressing her point. "That's just it. If Parker doesn't understand how important my family is to me, then maybe we need to rethink this whole thing."

"Meg. Come on, now. There has to be a way where we can

get to the bottom of this without going to such extremes. You're just upset, that's all," Frankie said.

Meg turned to address her friends face-to-face. "Based on what I overheard, my father may very well have an addiction to sleeping pills. Then there's my fiancé — who may have just made things worse. And now my girlfriends who are supposed to be on my side are encouraging me to suppress my feelings. What in the world?"

Meg watched their faces as they shifted from a look of concern to surprise. When Meg turned around her father stood wearing a stern expression as his flesh turned red. He then uttered words that pierced her deeply. "I came here to watch my daughter get married. It's something every proud father longs to be a part of. But, if my presence here is causing you this much grief, then maybe I should go."

* * *

"Dad, wait!"

Meg stumbled to catch up to him while partially in shock over her father's timing. Growing up, it had always been just the two of them after her mother's passing. From her early adolescent years they'd faced everything together and in her heart she didn't see why this would be any different. But, just because Meg saw it that way didn't mean much if her father didn't agree.

"Dad, please. Talk to me. We used to talk to each other all the time," she said, running out of breath. "Tell me what's going on."

She watched as her father stopped and began crying aloud. "Dad?"

Listening to his sobs was enough to break her heart into a million tiny pieces.

Placing her hand on his shoulder she said, "Dad, please. We can't help if you don't open up and tell us what's wrong. Quite frankly, you're really starting to make me nervous."

He smeared the stream running down his face. "I didn't mean for it to come out this way. Nothing should interfere or get in the way of your wedding day, sweetheart. I'm sorry. I'm so sorry."

Meg gently motioned toward a nearby bench. "Dad, you mean the world to me. And, if there's anything in my power that I can do to help make this thing better, then wedding week or not, I'm going to do it. Please — let's sit down and talk."

Meg eased onto the bench, waiting as he pulled himself together. But, it was the next words he uttered that truly caused him to fall apart.

"I blew through nearly half a million dollars in the last six months and Mariam has no idea. It was practically everything we had in our savings account."

She wanted to speak, but couldn't.

Her dad continued, "I thought I had it under control. I figured I'd borrow a little and replace it with more than I borrowed in no time. And, that's exactly what I did at first. Every time I won, I replaced the money with more than was originally there."

"Won what, Dad?"

"Poker. High stakes Poker. I'd take off every now and again with a few of the old guys from the job and go gambling at the casino near the racetrack in upstate New York. Not long after I retired, I had all this extra time on my hands and started feeling like I didn't have a purpose. I guess between my health issues and all — everything started feeling overwhelming. So I —"

"You gambled," she stated.

Her father nodded. "Small amounts at first. But, the adrenaline rush that came over me every time I'd win kept calling me back for more." His voice trailed off.

"And, how much did you lose again?"

"Around four hundred fifty. Maybe a little more — or a little less. Either way, it's not good," he replied.

Trying not to overreact, she said, "We all make mistakes, Dad. The more important thing is that you're honest with Mariam, and then you can come up with a strategy to fix it."

"Yeah." He chuckled. "Easier said than done. Somehow I had this bright idea that not only would I make enough to clear some medical bills, but maybe I'd even move us out here to get away from city life and live closer to my daughter. Boy, was I wrong."

She placed her hand on his. "Dad, two heads are always better than one. We can all put our ideas together and figure this out. But, I need you to be upfront with me. What's this I hear about you and the sleeping pills?"

Meg watched with a broken heart as her father held his head. With every tear that fell she knew he was in trouble. She hadn't seen him cry like this since the day her mother breathed her last breath.

"Meg, I don't know what I was thinking. I probably wasn't thinking at all. After I started losing large amounts the stress became so overwhelming that I couldn't sleep. I hid things so well from Mariam, but inside it was eating me alive. I still don't even want her to know now — at least not until after the wedding."

Meg shook her head in opposition. "No. Dad, I'm sorry but wedding or no wedding you have to break this ugly cycle. And, the only way you can do it is to come clean."

He looked up to the sky. "What if she leaves me over this?"

Meg thought for a moment. It always seemed like the men

in her life were made of steel, wearing such tough exteriors while facing whatever life threw at them. But, then there were these vulnerable moments — moments that reminded her that even tough men needed a shoulder to lean on.

"Dad, after all these years? Do you really believe Mariam would just up and leave? She may come up with a list of other things she'd like to do to you, but leave? I don't think so."

He stacked his hand over hers. "Thanks, Kiddo."

"Dad?" She sighed.

"Yeah?"

"Would you ever consider seeing someone about this? Maybe talking to a therapist could help you get down to the root of what's really bothering you."

Meg watched as her father leaned back, carrying the weight of the world on his shoulders. "I never considered myself to be one of those guys who laid out on a couch, talking to a shrink. But, maybe this time something has to give. I feel like I don't have a purpose or a place in life anymore." He then held his head down. "Honestly, I feel like a complete failure. Look at me. I flew out here to celebrate you and Parker, and I couldn't even make it through the week without ruining things."

She shifted, then looked into his eyes. "Do you remember what you used to tell me when I was younger? Whenever I failed at something, what would you say?"

The corners of his mouth began to curl. "Never let life get you down, baby girl. You got this." He chuckled.

"Yes, that's exactly what you would say. So, now I'm giving it back to you. Never let life get you down, Dad. You can get through this."

His eyebrows raised. "Thanks, Meg. I'll have to remind myself of that as I try and work up the courage to tell Mariam."

As Meg leaned over, giving her dad a hug, a familiar female

voice shifted the atmosphere. The sound of the waves faded, the sentimental moment subsided, and all Meg could hear was Mariam's voice echo in a stern manner.

"The courage to tell me what, Sam?" she asked.

Chapter 9

Nora

One long sultry kiss is all it would take to clear Nora's mind from the stress she'd left back in New York. At least that's what she allowed herself to believe. She'd already given herself permission to let her hair down about an hour ago, and had been successful at it after the broken heel incident. And, with a man at home who'd already divorced her emotionally — what would one little kiss do? It certainly wouldn't hurt Liam. And, it might just help make the pain dissipate — or so she wondered.

Nora extended her foot, allowing Chuck to slide a floral flip-flop in between her toes.

He explained, "The woman in the gift shop said it's one size fits all. I figured this would hold you over — at least until you get back to your room. Although, my hope is that you'd stay a while."

Stay a while? she thought. She'd stay all evening if he was going to continue to distract her, the way he'd managed to do thus far.

On the flip side, she was also cautious not to fall so quickly for the whole gentleman act. He was rather smooth in the way he ran to her aid so quickly — but he sure looked good while doing it. If this is how those so-called summer flings, or hot girl summers got started, then she was definitely intrigued. After all — being a rule follower all her life hadn't gotten her anywhere.

He slid on the second sandal and said, "Penny for your thoughts."

Nora smiled. "I haven't heard that in a long time. I was just wondering if you're always this debonair and smooth with the ladies."

"Hey, I was just trying to help. I saw a lovely lady in need and quickly figured out a way to meet that need. There's no harm in that, is there?"

In Nora's mind, this is how it always started with men. And even though she hadn't been on the dating scene in a long time, some things hadn't changed. A kind gesture here, a little buttering up there and before you know it he'd have her locking lips and doing all kinds of things she'd later regret.

He extended his hand. "Would you prefer that I take the shoes back?"

"No. You're actually saving me from hobbling around like an idiot. So, thank you, but I am happy to pay for them."

If he only knew that her mind was trying very hard to be cautious but her body was considering everything it shouldn't. Better yet, it was probably best that he didn't know. This had to be the grief, the heartache, and upset at its boiling point. It would soon simmer down - at least she hoped.

"Nora," he said, extending both hands this time. "I won't accept a dime. And, just so you know, I have a reputation around here, if that helps put you at ease. I used to be a full-time resident on the island until a promotion recently called for me to move," he explained. She didn't miss a word as he exposed his charming dimples.

He then offered, "You can feel safe around me. I promise."

She popped out of her seat, then twirled her foot around to display her sandals before replying, "Would you like to dance? I think they're playing my song."

One might wonder what song was playing, but not even Nora knew the exact answer. All she knew was it sounded like tropical island music and it helped set her mind free. And, to her that's all that really mattered.

Chuck's hand slid over hers, guiding her to the balcony where he swayed to the rhythm and the beat.

* * *

"Can I entice you to try another piece of my Guava Duff?" Chuck asked.

Nora glided her fork into her mouth savoring every bit of the delicious dessert. "Mmm, that butter rum sauce is amazing. And, the dough. You have to take this away from me. I'm a sucker for carbs." She laughed.

"Who isn't nowadays? Besides, their Chef is amazing. One more bite and I might have to loosen my belt," Chuck teased.

"Ha, my kind of guy." Nora spent time subtly loosening up around him, and she found herself wanting to know more.

"So, Chuck. Tell me about yourself and —" she nodded toward the inside of the B&B. "And, I think you mentioned something about knowing the history behind this place. I'd love to hear about that as well."

He slid his dessert plate to the middle of the table, offering more. "Let's see. Where do I begin? Umm, I lived here for about eight years prior to working with Parker. I'm originally from San Francisco, born and raised."

"Ah, I've always wanted to visit San Fran." She smiled.

"You should. I think you'd enjoy it. I started my career out there as a real estate agent, climbed the ranks, and somehow found my niche specializing in bank owned properties, or my favorite aspect which is helping clients out of tough situations before the properties are repossessed."

Nora sat back in her chair, folding her arms, finding herself more and more intrigued. "Wow, most look for opportunities to capitalize on other's weaknesses. It sounds like you do just the opposite."

"I definitely try. I can't say that it always works out. But, if there's ever a way I can help I try my best. Right now, my company has me working on Hilton Head Island in South Carolina to help expand their mortgage division. So far, it's been quite an adventure."

"Hilton Head? Wow. It sounds like you hardly have time for boredom. How did you manage to land another island job?"

His smile and charisma as he spoke about what he did for a living was infectious. But, in the back of Nora's mind she wondered about his kids, and his love life. Without any signs of a ring it created even more of a mystery.

Chuck cleared his throat. "Hey, the company sees an opportunity for growth in this niche market and apparently they think I'm the man for the job. When the boss says go, I pack my bags and head out."

"Makes sense." Then after a silent moment, she glanced from his ring finger and said. "I hate to be so forward but —" She hesitated.

"No worries. It's a question I get asked all the time." He held up his hand. "You're wondering if I'm married or have kids?"

She nodded. "You don't have to answer that if you don't want to."

"I don't mind. At fifty-two years of age one would assume I could check yes to both boxes, but that's actually not the case," he explained. "I was married once in my thirties. The marriage lasted all of two years before she decided to go back to her ex. I guess I wasn't her cup of tea. Or perhaps that applied to both of us, to be fair. For her, I think I was too much of the traditional, predictable, straight laced type. She needed more of a rugged, bad boy, or party type, so the marriage slowly but surely fell apart."

Her mouth dropped open. "You're kidding me, right?"

He laughed. "I wish I was. I couldn't make this stuff up if I tried. My parents raised me to be a gentleman. I truly don't know any other way. If that wasn't enough for her, then to be honest, I was happy to see her go. Since then, I came close to getting engaged once, but that was during a time when she was going through some hardships with her family, and relocating to be with me wasn't going to be an option. So — here I am. Fifty-two, alone, and in a relationship with my career."

Nora didn't know if the last part was a good thing or not, but she certainly could relate. She also would've never guessed his age. His body and his muscles didn't look a day over forty-five and his grays looked stylish and distinguished — just the way she liked it.

"Sounds very familiar."

This time he leaned back. "How so? I'd love to hear your story. As much as you'd care to talk about, of course."

Nora glanced at her watch. "Trust me, we'd need way more than a sit down over dessert to tell that story. Plus, I really don't want to bore you."

He folded his arms. "I've got nothing but time on my side. I'm here on vacation." He chuckled. "And, I'm all ears."

* * *

Two hours into their evening stroll felt like it flew by for Nora. She didn't want their time together to end. He was handsome, a good listener, and just as aggravated about her soon-to-be exhusband's actions as she was.

"Do you find yourself wishing you could pay him back?" he asked.

"I will, but I'm going to do it the right way. I'm calling my lawyer first thing in the morning so he can initiate the paperwork. It's not exactly something I wanted to focus on while I was out here, but I'm finding the sooner I get the show on the road, the better off I'll be," she said, then reached out to him.

"Hey, I owe you an apology. You invited me downstairs for dessert and for pleasant conversation. No man in his right mind would want to be around a woman who's going through something like this. I'd understand if you wanted to call it a night."

Chuck laughed. "Well, perhaps I'm not in my right mind then. I find your story to be heartbreaking, yet intriguing all at the same time. I guess there's something about it that drew me right in."

"Interesting. What part intrigues you the most? Would it be the hotel incident where he had the nerve to stand outside the room, trying to justify his extra curricular activities or the part where he came back to the apartment after she cut things off with him, seemingly appalled that I would even think about asking him to move out?" she teased.

The more Nora talked about it aloud the more empowered and emboldened she felt to proceed with the divorce. The mere disregard for all the years they were together made her question if Liam ever really loved her. Maybe the whole marriage had been a sham.

Chuck replied, "That's just it. You laugh, but it's guys like that who give the rest of us a bad reputation. They have absolutely no regard for their vows or the feelings of their spouse and it disgusts me. If I were lucky enough to have a good wife, I couldn't even think about making love to another woman. But, that's just my take on it." He turned to face her. "I can tell you're a strong woman. It's that same strength and tenacity that will get you through this. Even now at a time when you have every right to be an emotional wreck — you're out here allowing yourself time to grieve and clear your mind, which is wise. Most would probably just stay in the relationship out of the fear of change or being alone."

Rolling her eyes, she replied, "The only thing I'm fearful of is not getting away soon enough. I feel like a fool for not seeing it coming sooner." She shook the idea out of her head. "Regardless, there's one thing for certain — wallowing in my sorrows over a deadbeat marriage is absolutely pointless. We've been physically and emotionally separated long before now — so what difference does it make?"

Just then, Nora stumbled over an object causing her to fall sideways into his arms. "Oh," she called out. She tried to regain her footing while still leaning on his chest. "Two times in one night — I'm on a roll."

Every ounce of her being knew the right thing to do was to pull away quickly. But, the way he caught her and held her close — and the way she could feel the warmth of his spearmint breath was enough to make her forget about right versus wrong.

He smiled. "You're good. I won't let you fall."

Is it terrible that I want to kiss him? she thought. She felt like a teenage girl. Technically, he didn't ask for a kiss but if he came any closer, only God knew what she was capable or incapable of. Again, it had to be all the emotions trying their best to take her on a joy ride.

She responded, "I'm fine. It was probably a shell or something." Nora rearranged herself to look down at her foot. "Ooh, a very big shell. Surely, I can't leave this beauty behind. She's definitely one of a kind," she said, as she bent down to reach for it.

Mentally, she calculated the moment, labeling it as a close call and reminded herself that she was still in the midst of a fresh heartbreak. Trying to heal her wounds by indulging with an attractive man would solve nothing — *absolutely nothing,* she thought.

While admiring the various angles and lines of her seashell she heard Chuck calling her by name. "Nora."

"Hmm." She watched as his gaze drifted to the water.

"I know this is last minute, you don't really know me that well and — I'd understand if you declined."

She laughed. "Whoa. Why don't we start with the question before arriving at an official decline."

He slipped his hands into his pockets and looked her square in the eyes. "I was wondering if you'd be interested in joining me at Parker and Meg's wedding. It's at the B&B, so you wouldn't have to go far. And, I figured since we both like the beach and dancing, you might be interested in being my plus one — that's only if you don't have other plans."

"Actually, I've yet to hear the history of how this place came to be. Maybe you could share the story with me over dinner and dancing at the wedding," she replied. Surprisingly, the words came so natural, as if she were free from the burden of all that awaited her back home.

Extending a hand as he led her back toward the B&B he said, "Good then, it's a date."

Chapter 10

Meg

"The courage to tell me what, Sam?" Mariam's voice boomed.

Meg held her breath for what felt like an eternity as she watched her father's face turn red. Mariam circled around and stood before them.

Meg spoke, "I think it's best that I give you two some alone time." She then turned to her father. "I'll be in the main office checking on the arrangements for the rehearsal dinner if you need me."

"Meg, don't rush off on my account," Mariam begged. "Apparently, your father feels totally comfortable talking with you around. Meanwhile, I've been trying to console and support him for months, and I can't seem to get a single word out of him," she explained.

"Mariam, I wanted to talk to you," Sam said. "I just couldn't find the right words."

Again, Meg interjected, this time reaching for Mariam's hand to join with her father's. "Look, what matters most is the two of you are here now, ready to have a conversation that's been long overdue. And, while every part of my being would love to stay here and intercede, there's a wise man, who recently advised against it," Meg continued while looking downward. "I recently argued with that wise man, knowing deep down inside that he was right. Now, I need to go and apologize to him and make things right before our wedding," she explained. "And, you two need your privacy to talk things out."

Meg got up and began walking away before turning around one last time. "Mariam, just so you know — dad would normally never confide in me over you. He loves you, and as his wife you will always come first. I was the one who overheard your recent argument, and I'm the one who should apologize to you guys for prying."

"Sweetheart," her father pleaded.

"No, Dad. It's true," Meg surrendered, putting her hands up. "If you guys need me for anything — and I mean anything, I'll always be here. But, for now — I have a relationship to go mend." She pointed toward the B&B. "And, a wedding to get ready for. If you need me I'll be inside."

Meg backed away, giving them their privacy.

* * *

Inside Meg ran into Corrine. "There you are. How's everything going with the guests?"

"I told you not to worry. I have everything under control, including our special guest who appears to be having a really good time with Mr. Chuck." Corrine winked.

Meg paused. "Wait. What did you just say?"

Corrine smiled. "You heard me correctly. As we speak I believe Miss Hutchins is joining Parker's friend, Chuck on a little excursion. Can't say I blame the woman. I can't think of a better way to get over a lying, cheating son of a gun, than by getting back on the saddle and —"

Meg held her hand up. "How did they meet? Last time I checked she was staying secluded in her room, wallowing over her sorrows while ordering Chef Sean's tacos."

Corrine's smile grew. "I might be somewhat to blame. Although, the way he was looking at her I really don't think so."

"Corrine, what did you do?"

The last thing Meg needed was a failed matchmaking attempt to go wrong, ultimately agitating the one and only guest who had the ability to make or break their business.

"Don't fret, my dear. I just told her there was a gentleman who asked me to pass his business card along. Responding to the request was completely optional."

Corrine leaned in and whispered, "But, aren't you glad she responded. After being cheated on, Stella definitely needs to find a way to get her groove back, don't you think?"

Meg stared at Corrine before bursting into laughter. "If by Stella, you're actually referring to Nora, then yes perhaps it's a good thing that she's found a way to have a little fun. But, as for us — we are going to mind our business. I've already learned firsthand this week how poking my nose around in all the wrong places can stir up trouble. Now, on a completely different note, have you seen Parker?"

Corrine pointed toward the staircase. "He's upstairs. He came in sulking about an hour ago," she explained. "I'm not sure what's going on, but you might want to check on him. Oh, and before I forget. The flowers for the rehearsal were delivered and I placed them in the back office. If there's anything else you need, I'm going to the kitchen to pick up an order for one of our guests."

"Thanks, Corrine." Meg smiled

"No problem. Now, go upstairs and take care of your man."

* * *

Three firm knocks was all it took for Parker to open the door and walk away. Leaving Meg standing in the open space alone, without a greeting or a kiss showed Meg just how displeased he was.

"Hey," she said.

"Come in. Close the door behind you."

She watched his bare back as he slid a t-shirt over his head that matched with his cargo shorts. He then walked barefoot over to a loveseat, kicked up his feet, and made himself at home.

"I left Corrine in charge for the evening. Is everything okay downstairs?" he asked.

Meg looked back at the door. "Oh, yeah, she's fine. She's doing a great job, in fact. I came up here to check on you."

He chuckled. But, not the loving kind of chuckle he often gave when they were enjoying each other's company. This chuckle sounded as if it was backed with disbelief.

"Check on me? Why? I don't have anything to offer that's of value to you, Meg. Especially not my advice."

Tilting her head to the side, she said, "Come on, Parker. That's a bit much, don't you think?" She eased closer to where he was sitting. "I'll admit that you were right. I shouldn't have pried when I overheard Mariam and my dad arguing. But, I'm staying out of it now, and I'll only give my input if they ask for it. I've apologized and they're talking things over. That's a good start, right?"

Meg noticed him as he just looked at her. He didn't seem to be the least bit amused.

"What?" she asked.

"Nothing. There's nothing more to say. You apologized and made up with your dad. All is well."

Meg slid into the loveseat directly across from his. "All is not well because you're still mad. I'm admitting that you were right and I was wrong, Parker. What else can I say?"

He placed his feet on the floor and leaned in. "I don't want an apology or an admission, Meg. I want you to trust me. I would never do or say anything to harm you. Everything I have to offer and everything I ever do for you is always coming from a good place. If we're going to walk down the aisle together, I need to know that you trust me, even if you don't agree with me."

Shocked at his words, Meg was silent before saying, "I trust you with every part of my being."

"Really? Because it didn't feel like it the way you blew me off and stormed out of the room. You had to know that I didn't realize your dad overheard us talking. Plus, you also had to know that when I suggested staying out of their way — that was to protect your relationship with them — it wasn't an attack on you. And, I'd venture to say if we don't have that level of knowledge and trust with one another then what are we doing in the first place?"

Meg noticed the ticking sound of the clock that rested on his dresser. It was an indicator that the conversation had fallen silent, and the mood had taken a turn in a completely different direction than what she originally planned.

"What do you mean by what are we doing? I love you. And, I'm sorry I was so dismissive of your feelings. I really am. But, we're getting married, and I'm confident that what we're doing is right. I don't see why we'd start doubting that just two days before the wedding."

Meg followed his lips as he asked, "But, do you trust me?"

Without a moment to spare she got up and walked around the table positioning herself in front of him. Meg had always adored the way he looked into her eyes for reassurance of her love. This time was no different.

"I trust you to love me, and lead as the head of our household — I trust you to guide me and protect me. But Parker, I also trust that you know sometimes I will be hot-headed and other times I'm going to have an opinion that's different from yours. It doesn't mean I love or trust you any less."

His eyes dropped as he wrapped his arms around her leg. She found it kind of funny, actually.

"While my leg appreciates all the extra love and attention, it's my whole body that longs to have your hugs right about now." She smiled.

"I can give you a preview of what your whole body is going to get in just a couple of days if you'd like. Trust me, it's going to be way more than hugs."

"Parker Wilson!" she exclaimed.

But before she could reply any further he stood and engulfed her lips for as long as she would allow.

When they came up for air, she said, "You were starting to make me nervous for a minute there."

She felt his fingers tracing alongside her temple. "You have no reason to ever feel nervous around me. I'm in this thing for the long haul. I'd marry you right now if I could."

"Hmm, don't tempt me with a good time. We can always call Pastor and ask him to rearrange his schedule."

Meg left trails of sweet kisses on Parker's neck, his collarbone, and all over his lips just to make sure he understood how much she loved him too.

Chapter 11

Samuel

"I don't understand why you weren't upfront with me. I could've helped, Sam." Mariam's words hit like a bulldozer at the pit of Samuel's stomach. He wanted to be her strength, her pillar, her rock — not the guy who dragged their retirement savings into a bottomless pit. And, not the man who got hooked on sleeping pills to numb the pain. He felt ashamed.

"Baby, I —"

"Don't, Sam. Don't baby me now that the truth has come out like this. I've been there for you all along. I was there every day as you worked tirelessly on the job. I watched your health decline and helped nurse you back to good health. I even helped you through your challenges as you prepared to retire. I've been there through it all — but apparently that wasn't enough. You avoided talking to me altogether. If you were struggling, or in trouble, you should've said something. But to sit here and see you consoling with Meg, over me, especially after I begged and pleaded with you to tell me what was wrong — it hurts, Sam."

Looking up at his sweet wife's silhouette with water filling up in his eyes made him feel like a sad puppy dog. He had no choice but to come clean with her and explain. "It's not the way it looks, Mariam. You will always be my number one, and I think you know that by now. Meg, just happened to be in the right place, at the wrong time, and that's when everything came crashing down. As for you — you're completely correct. I should've come to talk to you. After I put in my retirement papers and threw in the towel, my days transitioned from feeling needed and being busy, to feeling hopeless." He folded his hands together. "I never knew how bad it would make me feel to watch the clock every day, wishing I was working on a case, or getting a call from the Lieutenant one last time. Sitting around watching the time pass, and losing track of what day of the week it is — well, that's going to take some getting used to."

Mariam sat beside him. "So, in the meantime, you decided to start gambling?"

"It's not as simple as you make it sound. When Kenneth and the old guys from the office started calling and inviting me to come out with them to the racetrack, and then to the casino, I had no idea what I was getting myself into. I really didn't. I kept saying to myself, what's one little innocent bet here and there, and what's one little innocent round of playing cards. If I could've seen what it would all lead to, I would've stopped while I was ahead."

Mariam nodded. "Problem was you couldn't stop. You were already addicted by then."

"Guess so."

He looked over at Mariam, and faced her. "And once the gambling spiraled out of control, I started losing sleep, which led to me getting hooked on the sleeping pills. But, I want you to know that I will do everything in my power to put every red cent back. I don't care what job I have to take. I'll be the only man in his seventies, mopping and scrubbing floors at the grocery store for all I care. I will restore our account — I promise I will."

Mariam folded her arms, seemingly in disgust. He waited, wondering if his wife of over twenty years could ever forgive his foolish decisions or if this would be the demise of their marriage. He couldn't blame her if it was. Sam had spent more time dedicating every part of his existence to the job when his attention should've been more devoted to her.

"Sam," she said in a monotone voice. "I care less about the money, and way more about your commitment to get help. You argued with me about seeing someone earlier. Now, will you change your mind?"

All the shame and embarrassment for the decisions he'd made, leading them to this point, took up residence in his mind. But, Sam didn't care anymore. His wife and the life they'd built together meant more to him then any gambling fix could ever accomplish. He only wished he stopped to think about that way before now. "Yes, my love. As soon as the wedding is over and we head back to New York — I'll sign up for whatever program. I'll do whatever it takes to get better again," he explained.

"Good," she replied, slapping her hand over his knee cap. "That's a good start. Now, I'm going for a nice long walk to enjoy the breeze. I'll be back in a little while."

He stood up. "I'll come with you."

"You'll do no such thing. I need some time to myself, Sam. I need to clear my head — alone. You've broken my trust. An apology is a start, but I need to figure out how to move forward without questioning everything little thing you say and do."

"But —" he replied.

"Sam. I'll see you back at the room."

* * *

* * *

Two hours had crept by painstakingly slow. Thoughts of how Mariam could stay away for so long without considering how much he'd worry, consumed Sam's mind. In a lot of ways he had no business seeking consideration from anybody. Nevertheless, he still wanted to put out an all points bulletin among the family, but something told him to think better of it.

The thing is — he believed the conversation earlier had gone well. Sure, confessing to his wife that he'd misused her trust and tried to self-medicate to ease the pain was no small matter. But, he loved Mariam and truly was willing to do anything to make it right.

The room door creaked open.

"Oh, thank God. I was starting to worry about you and was just minutes away from asking everyone to help me form a search party."

She slipped in quietly, closed the door and kicked off her shoes. "I just needed a little time to myself. No need to be up in arms. Here I am — safe and sound."

Mariam slid open the door to their balcony and eased into a nearby wicker chair. It didn't go unnoticed with Sam that she was responsive, but certainly not herself.

"What can I do to help ease the pain, Mariam? You don't know how terrible I feel for all the wrong I've done."

While staring outside, she replied, "You don't have to keep apologizing, Sam. I've been thinking about this and there's really nothing more to do except to wake up every day and pray to God for the strength to keep moving forward. It's the only thing that comes to mind at the moment."

"That's true, but I don't want this to create distance between us."

Sam went to the bathroom, grabbing the bottle of pills and

returned to Mariam. He took one look at the bottle, and then her. "Hand me that pen on the nightstand," he said.

"What for?"

"Mariam, just hand me the pen."

In one fail swoop he'd scribbled out his name and personal information, then tossed it over the balcony.

She gave him an earnest stare before asking, "How is loitering on the property going to resolve anything? For all I know, you could have a few hidden pills in your luggage and another stash waiting for you back home."

Sam hoisted the waistline of his pants and bent before her on one knee. "Do I have a problem? Yes. But, right now the only influence I'm under is my undying love for you. Please Mariam — give me a chance to regain your trust and in the process, don't shut me out. I need you, Mariam."

He held his breath for one whole minute waiting for her to utter the words. And, when she didn't he closed his eyes and prayed.

It was then that he felt the warmth of her hands take hold of his cheeks. He heard the words of her gentle and kind voice say, "For better or for worse. In sickness and in health, Sam. I meant it when I recited our vows to you back then and I still mean it now. But, I'm human. And, every once in a while I need to take a little time to pull myself together. Trust me, you wouldn't want it any other way. Understood?"

He nodded. "Take all the time you need. Just know that I'm here waiting with bated breath until the time comes when I can hold you in my arms again, and when everything will be alright."

Sam watched his wife get up and join him on the floor. Her stern demeanor had shifted, revealing a somewhat softer side as she kissed the curly hairs on his chest.

He chuckled, looking down at the button that had loosened on his tropical shirt. "I always was a bit of a hairy beast."

"Just the way I like my men," she said.

Before he could speak, he felt her soft lips kiss him again. This time on the side of his neck.

"Does this mean we're heading down the right track? As in — on the road to forgiveness?" he asked.

"It means even though my knuckle-headed husband did something very stupid, I still love you no matter what. It also means I'm still committed, even if I'm still mad at you."

Fighting the temptation to grin was darn near impossible. "I love you, Mariam."

"I love you, too. Now, hush up and plant a good one on me."

Sam considered how he'd gladly plant several good ones for the rest of his life as long as she'd allow it.

Chapter 12

Nora

Since sunrise, Nora laid in bed practicing the various ways she'd present her side to the lawyer. With the latest version she'd tossed around in her head — maybe she wouldn't try and drain Liam of everything he was worth. She already had a successful career, made good money, and didn't need a dime of what he had.

Besides, her time spent in paradise thus far had given her a new perspective on life. If all she was doing was waking up every day to work hard and constantly earn more — she wasn't living. At least not by her definition. Maybe it was time to turn over a new leaf.

It felt awful being the only one who cared about everything they'd built together as husband and wife. But, if he was willing to let it all go, in exchange for a god-awful affair in her opinion, maybe it was time she let it go, expecting nothing in return but her mental well-being and a fresh start in life. Speaking of a fresh start — the idea of enjoying another evening with Chuck was kind of nice. Not to be classified as serious, of course. Her heart wasn't ready for serious, but it was a nice distraction. And it gave her something to look forward to.

Her cell phone rang, breaking her train of thought.

"Hello, Liam," she said, letting out a sigh.

"Hi."

Silence hovered over the line.

While flinging the covers to the side, she felt the heat rising in her veins. *Would that feeling ever go away?* she wondered. Or would it steadily haunt her every time she heard his voice? Either way, she blamed herself for having that reaction — she probably should've never answered the phone in the first place.

He continued, "Not sure when you plan on returning, but I didn't want you to be shocked. The papers are all set to be served."

Clearing her throat, she said, "What?"

"The divorce papers, Nora. It's bad enough this thing is plastered everywhere for the world's consumption. And, yes, I already know what you're going to say. This was my fault and I'll take the blame. But, the way I see it there's no point in dragging this thing out. I made an appointment and ironed out the details with my lawyer. The sooner we get the proceeding underway, the sooner we can move on with our lives."

You son of a —She thought. But, since her ancestors raised her to be more dignified and show more class, she replied, "Well, well. How nice of you, Liam. I guess you call thismaking things easy for us? Or better yet, easy for yourself. I can only imagine just how much the details are geared in your favor."

Again silence flooded the line.

"There's nothing favorable about divorce, Nora. And, I'm not sure what kind of person you think I am, but it's not like I set out to meet another woman. I never intended for things to go this way. It took two, non-willing participants to break up this marriage, you know."

She retorted back. "I beg your pardon. That's an absolute lie and you know it. If I didn't want to work on healing our marriage then I wouldn't have been planning to surprise you with a trip to spend quality time together. A trip I'm currently on now — by myself!"

She flew open the curtains. "I also wouldn't have spent countless nights waiting for you to come home. But, none of that matters, does it? Your cold-hearted ways and lack of sensitivity is sooo unbecoming of you, Liam. I hardly recognize you anymore."

"Mm." He grunted.

"Let me ask you something. What did I do to cause you to turn on me and become so distant?"

Nora waited, and when he didn't respond she replied "Exactly. That's just what I thought. Your misplaced anger is unjustified. The bottom line is you did wrong — period."

The pivot in his tone shifted to strictly business. "The papers have to be served by an officer or a court official. So, whenever you get back in town let me know, and I'll give them the heads up."

Her mouth dropped open. One would think the public embarrassment was enough. But, if he thought he was going to send a cop knocking on her apartment door, making another public spectacle of their debacle, he had another thought coming.

She chuckled, but not in a good way. "Okay, Liam. You wait for that call." She then tapped the end button and powered down her phone.

The corner of Nora's mouth curled, realizing his timing couldn't be more perfect. She now had a strong change of heart and mind. The only legal transactions between them would be under her terms and her timing. If that meant she had to legally put up a fight, then she'd fight till the very end.

* * *

"I need another one of those tropical beverages," she confessed to Chef Sean, while perusing his breakfast buffet.

He smiled. "Is it that bad, my dear? It's only eight o'clock in the morning, but if you'd like to start with one of my fresh mimosas, then I'm happy to oblige."

Nora considered the idea, but then caved. "Who am I kidding? I can't hold liquor to save my life. Instead of embarrassing myself by getting wildly intoxicated, as tempting as that sounds — I think I'll stick with the carbs and indulge in the powdered french toast."

"Ah, excellent choice. And how about we wash it down with orange juice?" he said.

A gentleman's voice interrupted, "Please, make that two OJ's," Chuck asked, and then faced Nora. "I'll be joining the lady for breakfast this morning, if that's okay."

She gave Chef Sean the nod.

"A pitcher of orange juice can be found by the juice bar. If you need anything else, just holler for me," he explained.

"Thanks, Chef." Chuck waved.

Nora took a deep breath and without really meaning to she let loose, releasing everything that was dancing around in her mind.

"Chuck, listen."

With a look of concern he asked, "Is everything okay?"

"No, it's not. I mean — yes. Technically, I'm fine, but I think I should be very transparent with you. I'm in a very raw place right now. And, dining together, spending time around one another, and perhaps even going to the wedding together — I'm not sure it's a good idea."

His hands felt so secure as he placed them on her forearms. "What happened? Did something change overnight?"

She closed her eyes. "I talked to him this morning. And, after receiving a blatant verbal notice that he's waiting for me to return so I can be served with divorce papers, I just don't know that I'm in a good head space to —" She hesitated. "To do whatever it is that we're doing. Sorry, I'm not trying to make it sound so serious, but I just want to be honest with you."

He lowered his voice and was very direct. "The same way I want to be honest with you. I don't have any false expectations. I know you have a situation to handle back home. But, I'm having a good time with you, and if I'm not mistaken I think you feel the same way."

Nora nodded in agreement.

"Good." He rubbed her nose. "Then let's enjoy this weekend together. If you need a sounding board, I'd be happy to listen, or if you'd simply like to overindulge in carbs all day, I'm your man."

The burst of laughter that sprang forth from her belly was like much needed medicine to her soul. She liked Chuck. There was something about him that was genuine and oh-so refreshing.

* * *

"Hey, umm. There's something I should probably share with you — not that it really matters," Nora confessed.

She noticed Chuck wore powdered sugar on his mustache which she found to be funny and oddly attractive.

"What?" he asked, looking perplexed at her facial expression.

She motioned. "You have a little powder on your face. Actually, the look suits you very well."

"Ha! Forgive my manners. I blame it on Chef Sean for making this amazing spread," he said.

"It's definitely delicious." She laughed.

"So, what did you want to tell me?"

Nora folded her napkin and placed it carefully on the table. This was the part she dreaded most. For the last several days, she enjoyed being Nora Hutchins, a normal person like everyone else without all the glitz and glam that came with fame. However, if she continued on without revealing who she really was, then she feared the omission would soon catch up to her — especially at the wedding.

"I'm a news anchor. I work for America's top morning news show. Perhaps I'm not as recognizable without all my studio make-up on, but a lot of people know me as Nora Emmerson."

His eyebrows drew together as he sat back, taking it all in. "Interesting. I knew you looked familiar, but I thought it was just me. No offense, but I'm not much of a tv or a celebrity buff, soo —."

She laughed. "It's okay. I actually find it kind of refreshing. You don't know how much I've enjoyed just being normal with you. It's just — if we happen to bump into anyone at the wedding who refers to me by my real name, I didn't want you to be shocked."

"Oh, so you're back to attending the wedding, again? Good to know," he teased, and then said, "I thought you were going to make me fly solo, which is fine, but doing the whole single thing can be so overrated."

Nora cracked up in agreement. *Was the single-life overrated?* she thought as she laughed. She wouldn't know. Nora only knew that she didn't have a choice. Life was forcing her in that direction whether she cared to be there or not. The only thing she wouldn't accept was society's false labels about her newfound single status. She'd already been in circles with people who made comments like, 'Oh, you poor thing' to other divorcees or women who couldn't have babies. No way — that wouldn't fly with her. She wouldn't be labeled as anything less than strong, resilient, an overcomer, maybe even a middle-aged woman who was bad to the bone — but under no circumstances would she be referred to as 'poor thing.' *No, thank you!* she thought.

"Hey, as long as you don't try and hold me liable for making you look bad on the dance floor, then we're good," she teased.

He smiled. "Oh, really? Well we'll just have to see about that."

When the lighthearted banter settled, he continued, "I don't know how I missed asking you about your career. I apologize. I know you probably had to work really hard to achieve such success."

"Very hard," Nora said. "And, as crazy as it sounds, since I've been out here, I haven't had the desire to call in, to get back on the air... or to do anything really. Isn't that crazy?"

It was the one piece of the puzzle that didn't make sense to Nora. Her career had always been the one thing that helped get her through the hardest of times. With no one in her life except her husband, the job had been her support system, her best friend, and even her addiction at times.

Chuck continued, offering sound advice, "I have one word for you."

"What's that?"

"Trauma. You've been through a lot as of late. It's okay if things aren't exactly the same right now. Allow yourself permission to be different — to even feel different about things that were once familiar to you. It's okay."

She tilted her head. "Is it okay for me to feel like I don't want to go back? Is that even normal? Or better yet— is it okay for me to wish I could erase the last two decades and start a new life?" She waved her hand around. "Maybe in a setting like this. Away from the news station, away from my old life as I knew it, away from it all."

Chucked leaned in. "The only person who can answer that is you. You have to decide what will make you happy."

She thought about it. "I'm not sure what the outcome will be, but I know what would make me happy in this moment." Feeling surprised at herself, Nora began to smile.

"And, what would that be?"

"Take me on an adventure. We're surrounded by this beautiful oasis. Let's put all this serious talk behind us and have a little fun."

He let out an infectious laugh. "I didn't see that coming, but I like it."

Nora leaned in closer. "Good. Do you like snorkeling?"

Chuck leaned in even closer. "You are looking at the king of snorkeling. All I need to know is how long it will take for you to get changed?"

A devilish smirk washed over her face. "I'm wearing a bathing suit under this sundress. Last one to the shore is buying dinner tonight!"

Chapter 13

Meg

Meg scanned her eyes across the dining room, surprised, yet happy to see Nora out of her room spending time with other guests. She was even more happy to see Mariam and her father smiling again as they enjoyed breakfast by the balcony.

"Now this makes my heart happy. It's so good to see you two downstairs eating and enjoying one another."

Mariam reached out for Meg's hand. "You're just the person I wanted to see. I want to thank you, Meg, for everything you did. It means a lot to me."

"Thank me? I'm not sure how much of a help I was," she replied, shying away a bit.

Mariam continued, "I believe the exact opposite. It took your nudge, and your concern for your father to help bring things to light. Isn't that right, Sam?"

He nodded. "She's right, Kiddo. You embodied the kind of bravery I should've demonstrated a long time ago. And, because of that we were able to come together and talk things through. We even agreed on a plan to jumpstart my recovery when we get back. I'm not sure that would've happened if it weren't for you, so thank you, Honey. Also, we want to apologize. Actually, I want to apologize for putting a damper on things this week. It wasn't fair to you or Parker."

Meg extended both arms for a group hug and said, "Dad, none of that matters to me. I love you and would do anything for you. Our family is small, but precious in every way and you both mean the world to me."

She squeezed them, then pulled back to evaluate their plates. "Now, enough with all the sappy talk. I'm jealous. Your Eggs Benedict looks so good. If I didn't have a dress to fit into tomorrow I'd get some for myself."

Sam chuckled. "I'm almost certain Parker doesn't want his bride passing out as she makes her way down the aisle. How about you run and grab him so the two of you can join us for breakfast."

Meg winked. "Well, since you put it that way — I guess one little harmless egg won't hurt."

* * *

Later the same morning...

"Ladies, what would I do without you? It means so much that you could be here to support Parker and I for the wedding," Meg announced as she arranged the centerpieces for the rehearsal dinner. It was set to take place that evening. Frankie and Casey arranged the favors, while Parker's sisters positioned the chairs. With the rest of the Wilson family in town and staying at Savannah's house it served as a sign to Meg that the big day was finally upon her.

Lifting a finger to chime in, Frankie replied, "I think I can speak for everyone when I say that we wouldn't have it any other way. Plus, I absolutely love how you guys are keeping the wedding intimate and doing everything here on the grounds of the B&B. There's something about it that's —"

Savannah continued, "Cozy and romantic in an atmosphere that most can only dream of."

The corner of Meg's mouth raised, exposing her dimple. "Thanks. That's what we were aiming for. But, in reality, planning everything while still trying to the run the B&B was probably biting off more than either of us could chew."

Casey rested her hand on Meg's shoulder. "But, it's all coming together, so take a deep breath and give yourself some credit. As for the arrangements, everything is in place and you're practically ready to walk down the aisle. The only thing left on my mind is your dad. I saw you guys eating in the dining room this morning. Is everything okay?"

Meg placed the last candle on the table. "Thanks for asking, Case. He's definitely in better spirits than he was the other day. It's going to be a work in progress, but he's heading in the right direction. And to me, that's a very good start."

"Oh, good," she replied.

Frankie pulled out a chair, making herself comfortable as she displayed the tray of favors. "Um, on a much lighter note, on my way coming in this morning I spotted Nora Emmerson having a very good time with a gentleman friend. I don't know the details, but good on her for finding a way to move on."

Meg rolled her eyes wearing a smirk on her face. "Frankie, for Pete's sake. That guy friend of hers is Chuck Nesbit. He worked with Parker, helping him to get a great deal on the B&B. I'm sure he's just being cordial — and as you noted she's probably happy to have found something to do besides stay in her room the whole time. Chuck is attending the wedding, and then heading back to his own life in Hilton Head. Try not to make too much of it, okay?"

"If you say so," Frankie replied, gnawing away at her

chewing gum, but didn't look as if she believed one minute of it. "As her number one fan, I think I'm pretty good at reading her expressions. I could be wrong but, I think I caught a glimpse of a sparkle in her eye. It looked like wayyy more than two people passing the time. I'm just saying," she replied.

Meg noted to herself that she really needed to ask Parker to check in with Chuck. She wouldn't reveal those thoughts to Frankie, of course. If she did, she could expect to find her waiting for a minute by minute recap outlining every word that was exchanged.

"Frankie, the moment she checked into the B&B, we agreed to provide a service to Ms. Emmerson. A service that doesn't involve poking our noses into her personal life. So, regardless of whatever you saw and whatever is trending on social media, it's none of our business. Got it?"

Frowning like a child who'd been scolded, Frankie replied, "If you say sooo."

Deep down inside Meg was just as curious as Frankie was.

* * *

Later that evening, sitting in the presence of Parker's parents, his sisters Savannah and Allison, and her own family had already sealed the deal for Meg. Sure, tomorrow's exchange of vows would make their union official but they were already surrounded by what mattered most. Love and family.

Parker's mother raised her glass, offering the last speech of the rehearsal.

"I'm sure I'm not alone when I say that you two deserve way more than one night together to celebrate your wedding," his mother teased and nodded in agreement with those around her. "However, I also know that you have a B&B to run and you will carve out time this fall to enjoy an official honeymoon.

This leads me to the words of wisdom I wish to impart. Parker and Meg —" she said, glancing between the two. Never forget to carve out time for each other. Never forget to keep each other first. As you both already know, life will constantly throw you curveballs — but it's the marriages that keep each other first that win in the end," she said, raising her glass. "And to Meg, on behalf of the Wilsons, we officially welcome you to the family. My son's world changed for the better the moment he met you. May you continue to enjoy a lifetime filled with love and happiness together."

"Cheers," the group echoed. The sound of glasses clinking together solidified the special occasion.

* * *

That evening Meg and Parker completed their final rounds, checking on Corrine, Chef Sean, their guests and even their upcoming bookings.

"I can't believe this is it." Meg smiled, looking over at her soon-to-be-husband as they strolled down the hallway hand in hand.

Parker laughed. "Boy, you make everything sound so final. This isn't it — instead, it's only the beginning."

"You know what I mean. It's our last evening walking these halls as Meg Carter and Parker Wilson."

He stopped and planted the sweetest kiss on her lips. "I know exactly what you mean and I couldn't be more thrilled." He slid his hands around her waist "And to think, in less than twenty-four hours we will have pulled this off while still keeping this place afloat."

She traced her finger along his nose. "Yes. Of course, we couldn't have done it without Corrine and Chef Sean."

Parker pecked the side of her neck. "Since they're both

doing such a good job, maybe we should head out of town for an early honeymoon."

"Parker Wilson, are you serious? That's a surefire way to make them quit!"

This time he pecked the other side of her neck, sparking sweet distractions each time he did it.

He chuckled. "I'm teasing. But, by the fall I don't want to hear any resistance out of you. We're going away for at least one week. I'm already dreaming of all the things I'm going —"

"Now hold on there, tiger. We're less than twenty-four hours away from our wedding night. I think we can save all the details for then, don't you?"

He smiled. "I guess."

"Good. In the meantime, I'm technically not even supposed to be here. So, I'm going to give you a kiss goodnight and I'll see you tomorrow at noon."

A final long-lasting kiss reminded Meg of his love, the warmth of his touch, and his commitment to forever. When they finally parted ways, Meg grabbed her purse and followed Parker's lead as he escorted her to the car.

"Hey, Parker."

"Yes?"

"By any chance has Chuck mentioned anything to you about Nora Emmerson?"

"No. Although, we've been so busy running around here I'll admit that I've hardly had time to speak to him at length."

"Hmm." Meg pondered while reaching for her keys.

He continued, "Although, now that you mention it, he did seem like he was floating on cloud nine during our brief interaction at the dinner. I thought it was all surrounding the wedding buzz, to be honest. Is there something I should know?"

Meg shrugged her shoulders, then looked up at the stars as she replied, "No. A little birdie was whispering in my ear about seeing him with Nora. But — I'm sure there's nothing to it," she explained. She then pointed to the sky. "Look, there's a shooting star. I think we're supposed to make a wish."

Meg felt Parker's arm slide around her shoulders.

Hugging her a little bit tighter he said, "I already have my wish."

All she could do was melt into the fold of his arm, feeling thankful and blessed.

Chapter 14

Chuck

Around nine a.m. Chuck kicked his feet up in Parker's office, admiring his setup and how much he'd done with the place. Occasionally, he noticed his mind drifting to thoughts of Nora. Was he supposed to be thinking about a woman he'd just met? A woman who'd likely pack up her life and head back to what she knew to be reality. Perhaps it was the build-up of knowing she would be his date in a few hours at the wedding or maybe it was more. Either way, he'd try his best to maintain an even keel approach, allowing nature to take its course. Although, deep down he had to admit he hadn't felt this way in a while.

"Man, I'm so happy for you and Meg. You make starting over again look so attainable. You give hope to an old guy like me."

Parker's eyes perked up as he leaned back in his chair. "Oh, really? Well, that's good to hear. Although, I never took you as one who'd struggle with finding love. For you, I've always thought it was just a matter of time and meeting the right person, of course. Do you have any prospects lined up?"

Again Chuck had to resist the temptation to expose his inner thoughts. Technically, the answer was no. Chuck didn't have anyone lined up. He had only met Nora recently. There hadn't been nearly enough time to identify their feelings. And, before he knew it, he'd be back on a flight to Hilton Head, and she'd return to the big city. The only question that clouded his mind was — why did their time together feel so good? Why did thoughts of Nora linger well beyond the time they spent together? If only he knew.

"Me? Prospects? Ha, I wish," Chuck answered.

Parker nodded. "Oh, that's too bad. Well, the only piece of advice I have to offer — not that you asked. But, I'd say just keep an open mind and be yourself, Chuck. You're genuine, your heart is always in the right place. Heck, just look at the way you had my back with finding the B&B and introducing me to Mr. Barnes. There's no question you have a lot to offer. All you need is the right woman to show up at the right time. And, that usually happens when you least expect it."

Chuck smiled. "Like the way you met Meg at the beach house. Two people who found themselves unexpectedly at the same place, during the same period in time. One thing led to another, and before you knew it your worlds collided to the extent that you could no longer be apart."

"Uhh, yes. Except, the version I had in my mind wasn't nearly as eloquent or poetic — but yes, that's the idea," Parker explained, then rose from his desk.

"What do you mean?"

Wearing a smirk, Parker said, "Hollywood likes to paint a fairytale picture of what falling in love looks like. It's what sells. All they're interested in is creating one box office hit after another. But, I'm sure you already know by now that in real life, that's usually not how meeting someone and falling in love happens. Don't get me wrong, you'll meet someone every now and again who has a fairytale-like story, but it's rare," he explained, then opened up his window to a picturesque view. "Look at this for example. You see this setting out here? The crystal clear water, the perfect pink sand. People come here to find magic. Usually they're looking to fall in love, to rekindle what they had, or fix the things that are broken in their lives — and for some reason they think just being here will change their lives in a grand way and make everything all better. Well, I'm here to tell you — that's not the case. Love is not perfect and there's no magical atmosphere that can fix anything."

Chuck laughed. "Whoa. Is this coming from the same man who's about to get married in a few hours? You're starting to make me nervous, Park."

"You're darn right it's coming from me. Love is not perfect, Chuck. It's far from it. And, if you find yourself holding out and letting opportunities pass you by because you're looking for perfect, I'm advising you to quit while you're ahead. Meg and I went through a lot before we were able to get to this point. We both carried baggage from our pasts. She had an ex that put her through the wringer, and I was still grieving Jenna's death. I held on to the point of almost losing Meg to be honest. And, there was no perfect setting, no perfect Hollywood love story, and no perfect anything that would get us through those tough times. So — the moral of the story as I said before." He paused, drawing in a breath. "If you're at a point in your life where you're considering all the reasons why you haven't found love and you'd rather keep holding out for some fairytale moment, then you might just miss out on something real. Something that's imperfect, messy, and challenging, but also incredibly rewarding."

Chuck leaned back in his chair, taking in Parker's words. They struck a chord with him, resonating deep within his heart. He thought about Nora, the way she laughed, the way she looked at him with those piercing eyes that seemed to see straight through to his heart. He recalled their conversations, the easy banter that flowed between them, the way time seemed to slip away whenever they were together. It was true that he had only known her for a short while, but there was something about her that had ignited a flame within him. A spark he hadn't felt in ages.

As Parker's voice faded into the background, Chuck's mind drifted back to thoughts of Nora again. He couldn't deny the pull he felt towards her, the magnetic attraction that seemed to defy logic and reason. Technically, she was still going through a divorce. He probably had no right to be spending time with her at all. And, even if she wasn't going through it, was it too soon to be feeling this way? Was he just caught up in the excitement of their time spent together? Or was there something more substantial, more profound, hidden beneath the surface?

Chuck realized that he needed to be honest with himself. He needed to acknowledge the possibility that he might be developing feelings for Nora, even though it defied all logic and reason. He had always been the practical one, the guy who analyzed every situation, but love wasn't always rational. It didn't always follow a script or adhere to a timeline. Sometimes, it just happened.

Parker's words echoed in his mind, urging him to embrace the imperfect, to let go of the fairytales and open himself up to the messy, unpredictable journey of love. He knew that he had a choice to make – he could keep his emotions in check, chalk it all up to the excitement of the moment, and move on with his life. Or he could take a leap of faith, allow himself to feel whatever was blossoming between them, and see where it led.

As the morning sunlight streamed through the window, casting a warm glow across Parker's office, Chuck made his decision. He would go ahead with his plans to spend time with

Nora at the wedding, to get to know her better and explore the connection that seemed to be growing between them. He would embrace the uncertainty, the imperfection, and the messiness of it all, because sometimes, the most beautiful stories were the ones that weren't written in the stars, but in the unpredictable twists and turns of life.

With a determined smile, Chuck figured it might be best to warn his friend that he was bringing her as a guest. He turned his attention back to Parker, ready to be transparent. Little did he know that the path he was about to embark on would lead him to revelations he had never anticipated, and a journey that would challenge everything he thought he knew about love.

As he was about to speak, a rapid knock on the office door interrupted their conversation. The door swung open, revealing a figure that caused Chuck's heart to skip a beat. It was Nora, dressed in a simple yet stunning outfit, her eyes filled with a mixture of fear and terror.

Looking somewhat shaken, Nora said, "I'm sorry to burst in here like this, but you have to come downstairs. There's smoke coming from the kitchen, and I can't find Chef Sean anywhere."

As Chuck exchanged a quick glance with Parker, his heart began pounding in his chest.

Chapter 15

Nora

"I can't believe they made it," Nora leaned over, whispering in Chuck's ear as they sat and watched Meg approaching her groom.

The smoke incident in the kitchen had nearly altered everything. Chef Sean stepped away briefly to return a phone call to his daughter, and was certain he'd shut off all the burners. Unfortunately, he hadn't and that's all it took to nearly ignite the entire kitchen on fire. Thankfully, all was well as they sat and watched Meg and Parker hand in hand under the arched floral trellis.

Chuck whispered back, "It just goes to show that nothing can stand in the way of one's destiny. Those two —" He pointed. "They're destined to be together."

Nora digested his words. She once thought the same thing about her and Liam. Back when they exchanged vows, she thought they were destined to be together forever. But, after he cheated and slung her heart and her name through the mud, she now questioned everything.

She leaned over again. "Do you believe that we're destined to be with one person for the rest of our lives?"

"The truth?" he asked.

"I've heard enough lies to last a lifetime. Yes, the truth. Please, enlighten me," she whispered.

Nora watched as Chuck opened his hand, extending an invitation to hold hers. Without much consideration for how others around them would interpret the gesture, she slid her hand in his. It felt good.

He whispered, "I was always a one and done kind of man. The dating scene never did much for me. It didn't back then and still doesn't do anything for me now. But, just because we have our hearts set on being with one person for the rest of our lives doesn't mean it always works out that way. I'm a living testament to it."

In the background Nora could hear the words spoken by the pastor officiating over the wedding. She observed Meg's beautiful open back dress and acknowledged how happy they must be.

Again, she leaned in. "So, you don't believe that we're destined to be with one person for the rest of our lives."

"I didn't say that. I believe destiny looks different for everybody." He then turned and looked into the depths of her eyes. "I also believe that when you find the right person, you know it. And, in such cases, you better not ever let that person go."

It seemed somewhat ridiculous, or maybe just hard to fathom that she'd fly all these miles just to meet a real gentleman. His words ignited a flame, followed by raised goosebumps on her arms. Where had he been all her life? She could feel how sincere Chuck was when he described himself as a one and done kind of guy. If only she'd met him three decades ago before she gave her life away to someone else. If only things weren't currently so complicated.

Oh, well, she thought. *At least we still have this evening.*

"Now, repeat after me," the pastor announced. Nora listened as Parker and Meg recited their vows.

* * *

At the reception a lady with the most endearing smile approached Nora and Chuck. It was clear that she recognized who Nora was.

"I'm so sorry to interrupt, but I just had to come over and say hello. I am, by far, your biggest fan. And, while I promised the bride I would behave myself, I just had to come over and tell you how much I love your show."

"Thank you," Nora replied. "And, your name is —"

"Frankie. Frankie Jones. I catch your show every morning with a cup of coffee while getting ready for work. And, this wonderful man —" Frankie smiled, while waving for her fiancé over. "He can attest to my level of devotion to the Nora Emmerson segment."

Like clockwork, not only did Frankie's fiancé join them, but so did Meg and Parker.

Meg jumped in on the conversation. "If somebody would've told me that Nora was going to be a guest at our wedding I would've rolled out the red carpet or at least set aside a special table," Meg teased, then gave Chuck a funny look.

He smiled. "Yes, about that. I had every intention of letting Parker know, but then everything happened with the kitchen and —"

Parker chimed in, "No explanation needed. It just makes us happy to have the two of you here to celebrate with us. Ms. Emmerson, hopefully you've been enjoying your stay despite the little mishap earlier today?"

Nora looked up at Chuck, and then back to Parker. "First

of all, please call me Nora. And, yes. I've really enjoyed my stay. It was even better after bumping into this guy. He's the one who actually influenced me to get out and live a little." She smiled. "And, while a wedding was the last place I expected to find myself on this trip, I'm certainly having a good time." She glanced at Chuck. "I'm thankful to Chuck for inviting me to be his plus one. It turned out to be just what I needed. And, to Meg and Parker, thank you for reminding me of how beautiful and special love can be. I'd almost forgotten."

"The pleasure is ours. Meg and I are honored to have you," Parker replied.

Frankie lifted a finger. "Actually, the pleasure belongs to her number one fan. Just in case anyone forgot."

Of course, Frankie's candid adoration for Nora sparked laughter among the group.

* * *

The warmth of the evening breeze was enough to make Nora close her eyes as she listened to the sound of the waves. Nothing compared to the peace that washed over her as she listened to the ebb and flow of the water. Nothing calmed her more than sitting on the veranda, wishing her time at the bed and breakfast would never end.

The deep sound of Chuck's voice soothed her even more as he joined her in the adjacent chair. "A bottle of water for the lady?" he asked.

"Thank you, Chuck. Just in the nick of time. Another minute from now and the sound of the ocean would've put me fast asleep."

He laughed. "Yes, the water does have that calming effect, doesn't it."

"Yes, it does. I'm going to miss this when I return to New

York. If only I could capture the moment in a bottle and take it back home with me." She smiled.

"Hmm. I know what you mean. But, honestly I'm having a hard time thinking about my return. Our time together — well, it's been easy... and enjoyable."

She noticed him raising the corner of his mouth just enough to expose the sweetest dimple.

He motioned toward her as he spoke. "Actually, I'm having a hard time thinking about us going our separate ways. There aren't enough words to describe the way I feel when I'm around you. Seems kind of crazy, I'm sure. But, I don't want it to end."

She felt his warm hand slip over hers, causing her heart rate to pick up at an erratic pace.

He then said, "Perhaps this is a one way street."

With her eyelids gently closed, Nora slipped her fingers between his. "You're not alone. I want to explore the rest of this weekend together just as much as you do. I want to throw caution to the wind, but —"

Chuck interrupted, "No buts. We have something pretty special here. You and I both sense it. Why can't we extend our stay another week or two and just —."

"And just what, Chuck? Fall in love? It sounds like a fairy-tale, for sure. And, maybe under any other circumstance I'd oblige, but technically I'm still a married woman."

Nora could feel his eyes glance her way, but she continued to look forward.

"Yes, you are married to a dirtbag who has no regard for your heart. But, who am I to try and get in the way of you doing the right thing. I guess asking you to stay here a while longer would be selfish of me."

She sat up and looked him in the eyes. "If you would've asked me thirty years ago I would've accepted the invitation in a heartbeat. You're funny, you're charming, you actually care to listen to everything I have to say." She laughed. "Even when I'm talking about nonsense."

Nora slid her other hand over his, soaking up the moment, and remembering the touch of his skin. "My assistant arranged this trip for me. On the flight out here the only thing I could only imagine was ordering food to the room and spending every waking hour drowning in my own sorrows. You changed that for me, Chuck. And for that, I'll forever be grateful."

Nora watched as Chuck stood then extended a hand for her to join him.

Cautiously, she took hold of his hand and stepped ever so close as if they were about to dance. The only thing was — there was no music. Just the two of them, the sound of the ocean, and the gentleness of the evening breeze.

In a deep voice Chuck replied, "You had me from the very moment I laid eyes on you, Nora. Even in this very moment you take my breath away."

With mixed feelings and emotions, Nora replied, "I'm certain the moment we get back to our regular lives this time will be nothing more than a sweet memory. Tomorrow, I'll board an early flight heading back to the city, and shortly thereafter you'll return to Hilton Head. There's a life back home that awaits us. One that doesn't require you waiting around for a woman that comes with baggage and drama."

He stepped back for a moment. "Wait, you're leaving in the morning?"

Nora's heart sank. The beautiful symphony that once surrounded them was now stifled by her plans for an early departure.

Hanging her head low she replied, "I thought about it and made a decision to change my flight this morning. Not that I'm looking forward to returning by any stretch of the imagination. However, if I don't get back to New York, Liam will try and figure out a way to get over on me and I'll likely have to hunt for a new job. I haven't spoken to my boss or practically anybody for that matter. It's time I face this thing head-on and stop running."

Chuck subtly leaned against the balcony. "Wow, yeah I can see why you'd want to get back."

The look of disappointment on Chuck's face nearly crushed Nora to pieces. She'd love nothing more than to stay and further explore the endless possibilities with him. After all, he was the man who found her when she was at her lowest and helped revive her... helped her to live again... to laugh again... and to feel again. But, how could she? How could she go down that road with a divorce proceeding lingering in the back of her mind? Technically, she wasn't even single yet. Was she secretly hopeful that Liam would change his mind and come back to her? *Not at all,* she thought. But, this was still one chapter in her life that needed closure. And, Nora Emmerson intended to deal with it the right way.

She took a step forward and embraced Chuck's face between her hands, then closed her eyes touching nose to nose and whispered, "Thank you, Chuck. Thank you for making me smile again. Thank you for showing me that there's potential to lov—" but she stopped herself. In her heart she knew it wouldn't be fair to unlock that floodgate of emotions, even if it was what she was feeling.

Chuck leaned in close enough where she could feel the warmth of his breath on her ear lobe. "Even if you can't say it, just know that I feel it too."

Chapter 16

Meg

After their first evening as husband and wife, Meg and Parker awoke with a new cadence to their morning routine. There would no longer be days filled with running the B&B and then returning to separate residences. There would no longer be long days serving guests and then ending with lonely nights. For Meg, packing her last few boxes and moving them from Frankie's house would be the start of something brand new.

At the B&B Meg raised a glass before friends and family who gathered for brunch. "Parker, I don't know about you but I think this moment deserves a toast. I knew when we planned to have our wedding here at the B&B it would be nothing short of amazing. But to look around and have your parents, your sisters, my parents —" Meg paused for a second and smiled at Mariam. She realized it was the first time she'd referenced her as a parent, even after all these years. In a loving way, she'd always been Mariam. She didn't love her any less, but her ties to her mother who had long passed made it difficult to say those special words, until now. Meg watched as Mariam turned flush.

She then adjusted her gaze to everyone else and continued, "And all of our wonderful friends gathered here. Gosh, just being surrounded by so much love gives me goosebumps. I just want you to know how much I appreciate you all being here," she said, then tapped glasses with Parker, who chuckled. "And, we would be remiss if we didn't give a big hand to Ms. Brown and Chef Sean who to this very hour are working tirelessly behind the scenes. Thank you for holding down the fort for us. We couldn't have done it without you."

Chef Sean, teased, "Except for the part where I nearly burned your kitchen down. I'm sure that's one event we could all do without."

Parker nodded, pointing in his direction. "Touché."

Then Casey, Meg's best friend from childhood spoke up. "I don't know about anybody else, but the fun doesn't end here. We've yet to see the rest of the island and we have energetic little ones who are anxious to get out and explore. I say we all grab a bite and then get out and see what Harbour Island has to offer."

"Here, here!" everyone cheered.

* * *

Once the buzz simmered down and everyone carried out plans, heading in different directions to explore, Meg and Parker remained at the B&B with the guests and Chuck.

Meg had already assisted Nora with an early check-out that morning and made arrangements for a car to take her safely to the airport. Now, the only thing left to address was Chuck who was making a poor attempt to hide his disappointment.

"Do you mind if I join you?" she asked, watching as he gazed out at the ocean over his half-eaten plate of food.

"Sure," he said, gesturing for her to take a seat. "I'd be

honored to have Mrs. Parker Wilson join me. Even though I still can't figure out for the life of me why the two of you aren't somewhere on a secluded island, enjoying your honeymoon."

Meg chuckled. "I know. Everyone has been getting on our case about it. And, trust me, it will happen in due time. But, Parker and I are still rather new at running the B&B operation." She motioned toward the sea. "Plus, we have our own special slice of heaven right here on this beachfront property to hold us over. Don't you worry. We'll make plans to go on our honeymoon very soon."

"Good. I'm going to hold you to it," he replied.

"Mmm." Meg smiled. "And, what about you?"

He drew his eyebrows together. "Me? What about me? I'm having an amazing time. The ceremony was beautiful, I managed to work on my tan, go on an adventure or two and well — what more could I ask for?"

Meg tilted her head slightly. "Really, Chuck? Is that all you have to say for yourself?"

"Yes. What else is there to say?"

Meg thought long and hard about how far she wanted to push the matter. After all, she was just a bystander who'd made a couple of observations at the wedding, but she was also no fool. Sometimes men simply didn't like talking about this sort of thing. *Maybe it makes them feel too vulnerable,* she thought.

Deciding to be brave, Meg said, "Look, I don't mean to pry—"

"But," he replied.

The corner of her mouth raised slightly. Then she raised her hands in surrender. "Hey, I can keep what I'm thinking to myself. I won't say a word. Just checking on you to make sure you're okay, that's all."

He glanced at her, again altering his brows. "Go ahead. Say what's on your mind."

After taking a deep breath and exhaling, Meg opened her heart. "You're disappointed that she's gone, aren't you?"

She watched as Chuck slowly nodded his head up and down. "Is it that obvious?"

Meg winced. "Just a tad bit. I didn't realize the two of you really hit it off so well. Not until last night, of course."

"Mm. Yep. It was a whirlwind, for sure. You can only imagine why her sudden departure hit like a ton of bricks. Guess it was my fault for allowing myself to —" He stopped.

Meg gave him a moment, and then replied, "But, I'm sure you already know about everything she's going through. I'm sure you've heard. It's all over the media."

While still staring at the ocean Chuck pointed his finger with an air of I don't give a damn, up to the sky. "You see, Meg. That's just it. The one thing people don't know about me and something they'll never understand is — I could care less about what's going on in the media, I could care less about the news, and I could care less about who's posting something on whatever platform people are using nowadays. I'm normally so busy I barely have time to pay attention to it anyway. I didn't know anything about Nora Emmerson, the celebrity. All I know is, I met a wonderful woman who made me contemplate what it would be like to love and be loved again — that's all. Period."

Meg's heart nearly stopped after hearing those words. For the first time she'd come to realize their interaction together was far more intimate than she originally suspected. He actually developed feelings for Nora. And, in that case, the fact that she was no longer there actually made Meg feel kind of sick for him.

Chuck continued, "Look. I'm not totally oblivious. I know she's a married woman who had to get back to life as she knows it so she could take care of everything, including her divorce. And, I would've never violated their vows and crossed the line with her in any way. But, there's something about her that was special, Meg. She was definitely one of a kind. But, I guess none of that matters. Not now, anyway."

Meg glanced down at her new wedding ring, completely understanding what it felt like to meet the right one.

Chuck repositioned himself. "I guess this all seems kind of ridiculous. As a man in his fifties, I've already been blessed to love in my lifetime. And, what I learned from that experience is that forever isn't for everybody. Soulmates and second chances aren't for everyone. You and Parker have something real special and something that's rare nowadays. If you know like I know, you better hold onto it and never let go."

Meg leaned in. "But, Chuck. Just because Nora had to go back to New York doesn't mean this is over for you two. Maybe you just need to give it some time."

He placed his napkin on his plate. "I'm too old to be chasing dreams, Meg. At least not these kinds of dreams. Business goals, travel, real estate, sure. But, this. I'm not cut out for this."

Chuck then switched gears as if reprogramming himself never to feel again. "Listen, you and Parker have been amazing hosts. I absolutely love what you've done with the place and I'm looking forward to getting back here as often as I can to visit. But —"

Parker walked up to the table, interrupting their conversation. "There's my lovely bride." He then shifted his attention toward Chuck. "Thank you for keeping the Mrs. company, but I may need to steal her away for a little while. I planned a small post wedding day excursion just for two."

"Now, that's what I like to hear. By all means, don't let me get in the way of your plans. I was just heading up to my room to start packing," Chuck explained.

"But, Chuck," Meg pleaded.

However, he wouldn't hear of it. She watched as Chuck folded his napkin and pushed back from the table. "The only word I want to hear from you is bon-voyage." He smiled.

Chuck leaned in, giving his good buddy a hug, then offered the same gesture to Meg.

"Thanks for inviting me out here to be a witness to such a beautiful wedding."

With a surprised look, Parker said, "Wait a minute. You're leaving early, too? If my memory serves me correctly, you had at least another two days scheduled on the books."

Chuck patted Parker on the shoulder. "I know, and I'm more than willing to stay if you guys need me. But, more than anything I think you two need some alone time, and I have a ton of work waiting back at Hilton Head for me. The sooner I get to it, the better."

After an exchange of final words and goodbyes, Meg and Parker watched Chuck head upstairs leaving the two of them behind.

"What just happened?" Parker asked.

"Well, let's just say he could probably use a friend right about now. It might not be a bad idea for you to head upstairs and keep him company while he packs."

"Mm, I'll go check on him. But, I'm giving it thirty-minutes, tops. Then, we have a little date planned. Just the two of us."

Meg closed her eyes, taking in a sweet, sultry kiss from her husband. "I'll be standing right here, waiting for you."

Chapter 17

Chuck

After three months of being buried knee-deep in bank owned properties, Chuck found himself just as worn and depleted as he'd ever been. Some days he wondered what was the point in living in Hilton Head, South Carolina if all he was going to do was miss out on everything it offered. One would think he hadn't emerged from his office or traveled all year. Even Harbour Island was starting to feel like a distant memory. Well, except for the parts that included Nora. After their unforgettable time together, she'd been pretty hard to forget. Since then, they'd only exchanged a text message or two — each one leaving him yearning to say much more. However, logic led him to restrain.

Chuck gazed at the time capsule on his desk, flipping it over as he'd done so many times. It was a gift from a former boss who was always adamant about what it stood for. He could hear the co-workers voice as she graciously said, *Every day we're gifted twenty-four hours on the clock to hustle and increase revenue for the company.* It was her go to phrase which he'd memorized by heart. Of course, Chuck always struggled with the concept. Surely, within those 24 hours, he'd dedicate the appropriate amount of time to the business, but what about the rest of his life? Was he just allowing it to pass him by?

* * *

His gaze was interrupted by the swift drop of a newspaper on his desk. A typical move made by Wyatt when he was upset. He was one of Chuck's closest buddies at the company and didn't mind expressing himself when he was agitated.

Chuck sighed. "Wyatt, did it ever occur to you that I might actually be busy?" he asked.

"That's what you call it nowadays?" Wyatt asked. When you're busy it usually involves taking calls, or clanking away at your keyboard. Fidgeting with your time capsule — that's just something you do whenever you're mentally checked out. And, believe me when I tell you, this is no time to be checked out, my friend." He shoved the paper closer, pointing out a section circled in ink.

Chuck always had an appreciation for Wyatt's work ethic and style. He had an old-school way of thinking, but was sharp, and innovative. And, he had an appreciation for simple things like reading a newspaper, which seemed to be a lost art.

"Wyatt, let me guess. You've been hovering over the auction section again, getting all fired up about the properties we couldn't recover."

"You're darn right I'm upset. Those folks down there at the bank are ruthless. I've been chasing after them for days about the one over on Dunwoody Lane. Do you think anyone ever got back to me? Absolutely not! They sit on the property files for months, and to no avail. Meanwhile, we could be helping more people recover or at least dig their way out of these situations before the properties go to auction to begin with." He sighed. "I'm starting to feel like my efforts are purely a waste of time."

Chuck nodded. "I get it, Wyatt. But, unfortunately that's only one aspect of what we do. I'd try not to let it frustrate you so much. Just knowing you're doing your best ought to count for something."

"Mmm."

As Wyatt groaned, Chuck closed the newspaper, finding himself nearly paralyzed over the front page headline.

In the background Wyatt continued ranting. "It's just so aggravating. Sometimes I feel like marching right over there and giving them a piece of my mind. It wouldn't be the most unreasonable thing I've ever done. Would it?"

Still frozen in disbelief, Chuck read the subheading for a second time. *Nora Emmerson Proves to Be Victorious in Divorce Hearing.* "Crazy," he whispered softly.

Wyatt continued, "I know, it's crazy. Somebody should be holding them accountable instead of allowing them to sit on their laurels all day."

"No. I — I mean, yes. I agree with you. But, we need to revisit this later on, Wyatt."

Chuck stopped glaring at the paper long enough to search for his car keys.

"We can pick up with this next week, I promise, but for now, I have somewhere I need to be."

Poised with a look of concern, Wyatt belted out, "Next week? Are you nuts? Where are you going?"

Chuck gripped his keys in one hand and flung his sports jacket over his shoulder. "I have some unfinished business in New York to take care of." He paused, giving Wyatt a hardy pat on the shoulder. "And, to answer your question — yeah, I'm as nuts as they come. A certifiable nut to be exact. I'm stepping out on a limb and taking a risk, Wyatt. In the end it will either be the best thing or the craziest thing I've ever done. Hopefully it will have all been worth it."

"What?"

Chuck smiled. "You heard me. I'm heading to New York City. Hold down the fort until I get back." He began walking off before turning around with an even bigger smile. "Oh, and by the way. Thanks for the newspaper. It made my day!"

* * *

"I'd like to purchase a one way ticket to New York, please." Chuck asked, smiling nervously while digging for his cell phone.

"Sir, which airport? Laguardia, JFK, Newburgh, Westchester County —?"

He watched as the woman methodically smacked on her chewing gum while waiting for his reply.

That's when it hit him. His spontaneous plan was probably not as carefully thought out as it should've been. Other than knowing that her studio was located in Times Square, he had nothing. "Um, which one will get me closest to Manhattan?"

With a slight look of annoyance, the clerk clicked away at her computer. "Your best bet would be Laguardia. And, from what I can tell we have a flight pulling out of here in an hour."

"I'll take it," Chuck replied, then slid his card across the counter.

After walking down the long corridor and clearing the security check-point, Chuck dialed his dear friend, Parker.

"Hello."

"Parker, this is Chuck. You got a minute?"

"I have several minutes for you. How's it going, man?"

Releasing a breath, Chuck said, "Oh, it's going. I'm actually calling because I need you to talk me off the ledge."

"Whatever it is can't be that bad. You're the most level-headed, logical person I know."

Chuck laughed. "Right. Except for today."

"How so?"

He glanced around the panoramic view of the airport, noticing a mom walking by with her toddler in tow, a magazine shop, and in front of him flight 3197 heading to Laguardia. "Well, I am currently waiting to board a flight to New York to try and win over a woman that I can't seem to live without. The only problem with this whole scenario is she has no idea I'm coming. So, technically this could either go well or go south real fast."

His comment was met with silence. "Park, are you still there?"

After clearing his throat Parker replied, "You read today's headlines, didn't you?" He chuckled.

"Yes, the bold face letters smacked me right in the face first thing at work this morning. Park, I've been holding back long enough. Messaging every now and again simply won't do. I haven't been able to get her out of my mind since the day we departed."

In his voice of reason, Parker spoke with certainty. "Okay, but hold on a second here. Let's really think this through. I have your back no matter what, but have you thought through how it would make you feel if she let's you down? Especially after traveling all that way."

Chuck thought long and hard about what his friend was proposing. He found a chair just a few feet away from where his plane would board and made himself comfortable. "I'd feel awful."

"Now we're talking," Parker replied.

"But — I'd feel even worse at the thought of not trying. Trust me, Parker. I considered picking up the phone and just spilling my heart out to her time and time again. But the timing never seemed right. And, now that she's free, I honestly believe that some things just ought to be said in person. If I fly up there and she wants to have nothing to do with me, then I'll know that my hunch was wrong, and I can move on. That's after I pick the pieces of my heart off the ground, of course."

"The two of you did have a special spark. If this is the way your heart is leading you, then I say go for it," Parker offered.

"Really? So, even though this feels like the most nonsensical thing I've ever done —"

Parker interrupted, "It doesn't make a difference. I say go for it. And — if there's anything that Meg and I can do to assist, we're all in. Just say the word."

"Well, now that you mention it..."

Chapter 18

Nora

Early the following morning, Nora did her usual prep for the show. A five a.m. workout, followed by a light breakfast and car ride into the office. Once there her television makeup would be applied, and her sweet assistant Camille would talk with her, going over the rundown for the day, one last time.

"Nora, are you sure you won't change your mind?" Camille asked. "I don't know if America can handle the idea of not waking up to Nora Emmerson every day. The morning news will never be the same."

"America will be just fine, Camille. Besides, the new anchor slated to take over is young, has fresh ideas, and will help lead the network in a new direction. It's a win-win for all."

Nora caught a glimpse of Camille's unenthusiastic facial expression. "What? You don't agree?"

"No. Not at all. The guys are already chomping at the bit to see who'll get promoted to lead anchor. If you ask me I think they're secretly taking bets to see how long the new girl will last."

Nora waved, nonchalantly. "Oh, what else is new. It was that way when I first started. Us women have to work extra hard to prove ourselves worthy, but if you're relentless, and put in the hard work, eventually it will pay off."

"Mm. Well, we'll see. I'll have to keep you posted. But, in the meantime, I still can't get past the idea that you won't be my boss anymore. I mean — what are you going to do? How are you going to fill your time now that you won't have to rise up at the crack of dawn to be here anymore?"

Nora swiped through her phone as her stylist applied the last curl to her hair. She paused, seeing a text message from Chuck, but chose to check it later. "I'll wake up whenever my body tells me it's time to get up." She nodded. "And, I'll stick to my workout routine, and figure out the rest as I go. I wish I had more to offer, Camille. I really do. All I know is it's time for change. I'm entering a new season and I can sense it just as clear as I can see you standing in front of me. It's time for me to move on."

She felt a heavy weight rest on her heart as Camille held her head down. But, it was what Camille said next that really hit home.

"I'm happy for you, Nora. You deserve this time to figure your life out. But, I can't help but think if it weren't for the divorce, you'd still be right here, tomorrow morning, doing what we do best."

Nora leaned forward, reaching her arm out to Camille. "I'm sure of it. And, that's also the very reason I have to go. I know there's something bigger and better waiting out there for me. Unfortunately, I had to get hit by an unexpected curveball to figure it out, but I'm not upset. In fact, I'm as happy as I can be. It's moments like these that present the perfect opportunity for change."

Nora allowed her hand to slip down as she motioned for Camille to have a seat.

"I actually owe you big time for everything you did for me," Nora explained.

"Me? Nora, I didn't do anything except my job. You were the one who taught me so much and inspired me to go back to school to pursue journalism. I'm the one who owes you, not the other way around."

Nora chuckled, then took a moment to recall when Chuck rescued her from her broken heel. As random as the thought was, it warmed her heart to think of the way he bought her a pair of replacement sandals, the way he held her when they danced. All sweet thoughts, of course. All memories she would've never created if it hadn't been for Camille.

"You, my dear, are one of the reasons I feel so free, and bold, and brave enough to start this new chapter."

"Me?" Camille asked.

Nora nodded with her eyes closed. "Yes, you. If it weren't for you booking my trip to Harbour Island, I would've hidden in my apartment with a gallon of ice cream while drowning in my sorrows. But, because of you, I was able to go on the trip and live — and you know what?"

"What?" she asked.

"It felt good. Darn good!"

Camille clasped her hands together and said all the things she normally would to be supportive of Nora. They really had so much more than just a work relationship. They were friends now more than ever. And, in Nora's heart, Camille would definitely be missed.

"Oh, my gosh." Camille dabbed the corner of her eye. "Nora, who knew? I had no idea such a small gesture could mean so much. At the time we were just planning for you and —."

Nora smiled. "I know. But, I returned a better woman for it. I have absolutely no regrets. Only good memories. So, thank you."

The two hugged long enough for Nora to close her eyes and thank the heavens for all the fond memories. Memories created on air, memories of her and Camille, and even memories of her time on Harbour Island.

She then perked up, wiping a tear from her eye. "Okay. Now, listen. We have to pull it together or else you'll have me looking like a raccoon on my very last show. I can just see the headlines now."

Nora grabbed her notecards and held them up. "How do I look?"

"Fabulous, as always," Camille replied, offering a thumbs up.

"Thank you. Now, for the last time, let's get out there and show 'em how it's done."

* * *

With the clock counting down until Nora was live on air, she poised herself, ready to deliver the best darn news segment of her entire career. She had spent over two decades serving the public with breaking news, revealing the truth, and touching hearts all around the world. She was humbled when asked to take on the position and now even more humbled as she prepared to let it go.

"It's so wonderful waking up with you, America! As many of you may have already heard, today will be my last day serving you from behind this news desk. Before I get into today's headlines, I'd just like to say how much of a privilege and honor it's been to wake up every morning with you."

As Nora spoke from the heart, she couldn't help but notice a tall figure standing just beyond her producer and the cameraman. Ordinarily she'd pay it no mind. Pertinent staff members took their position, practically running the entire show behind the scenes all the time. With all the bright studio lights shining in her direction she could hardly make them all out anyway. But, this particular gentleman — he was different. She couldn't make out his face, but he stood holding a sign in hand which made her even more curious.

"Now onto today's top story..." she uttered with her voice trailing off in the end.

Nora continued reading from the teleprompter sharing one riveting line after the next. But, it was what happened next that left her absolutely speechless on live television.

The man who she could now identify as Chuck stepped forward, holding up his large white sign.

"America, I apologize. Due to technical difficulties, we need to take a quick break. We'll be right back."

Now, Nora was used to fans gathering outside, holding up their attention grabbing signs, and eagerly waiting to participate in the day's events. But, Chuck? In the studio? She was shocked he hadn't been stopped by security, and even more shocked to see the camera was still rolling.

The sign read, 'Nora Hutchins, this may sound absolutely crazy, but I don't want to live without you in my life. Will you give us a chance?'

She mouthed every word of it before giving the cameraman a signal. Flashbacks of a text message that was left unanswered played through her mind, along with their last conversation, and the look on his face when she said goodbye.

"Chuck, is that you?" She watched as he approached the

desk, leaving the rhythm to her heartbeat in pure disarray. Had Nora forgotten about their feelings for each other since she left Harbour Island? Of course not. However, with all that had transpired since she'd left, it was reasonable to expect that he would move on.

"It's me." He looked around for a moment. "Standing here in these bright lights looking like a ridiculous fool." He smiled.

"Oh, my gosh. No — you do not look like a fool. But, you do have me wondering how you managed to make it inside the studio," she replied.

He chuckled, then glanced at the producer, then Camille. "That's a long story which we'll have to save for after the show. Look, I have so much that I want to say, but you have a show to finish, and I promised these guys that I would be quick. Do you think you'd be able to spare a little time to chat with me when you're off air?"

Nora glanced at her producer who was signaling the time. She then looked into Chuck's eyes, remembering just how sweet it felt to be heard, and to be in his arms. "Sure, of course. But, Chuck."

"Yes?"

"Before you go. I was wondering. Do you mean it? What you wrote on the sign," she asked, glancing down at his poster.

"I haven't been able to stop thinking about you since the day you left, Nora. When I wake up in the morning, while I'm at work, even when I try to keep busy — you're still on my mind. You did something to me back on Harbour Island. And, whatever it is, I want more of it."

In the background a voice began counting down...ten... nine...eight.

Chuck whispered softly, "I'll see you after the show."

She could feel a sweet kiss planted gently on her forehead, then watched as he was escorted to the back by Camille.

* * *

"Camille, all that time I spent pouring my heart out and you knew he was going to be here?!" Nora said. Her voice started off like somewhat of a controlled whisper that eventually escalated. "Would somebody care to tell me what's going on?"

If Nora were being honest with herself she really didn't care how it all came about. She was just as happy to see Chuck as he was to see her.

"Sorry, boss, but you have our producer to blame for this one. It became news to me the moment you walked into the studio. And, while I'd love to probe and ask tons of questions, there's a really good looking man by the name of Chuck waiting in your dressing room. So, you might want to hurry along."

Still speechless, Nora adjusted her clothing, then walked down the corridor to the tune of clapping, chanting and smiling faces as the staff congratulated her.

"We're going to miss you, Nora," someone called out. "Way to go on the last show."

And — while she heard it all, it was the build up and anticipation of what was waiting in her dressing room that held her attention the most.

Nora exchanged hugs and kind words with a few until she finally reached her door.

A sports jacket, denim jeans, and a white button down shirt didn't look nearly as good on anyone else as it did on Chuck. As he stood surrounded by dozens of red roses she was awestruck.

The unforgettable sign that he presented rested against her mirror.

"Congrats." He smiled.

Struggling to hear beyond her racing heartbeat, she replied, "Thank you," then looked around.

"Chuck, I can't believe you did all this for me."

"It's not nearly as much as you deserve."

The words struck a chord. It had been a long time since someone considered her needs and what she deserved.

"Nora, there's no point in me holding back. Not now. Not after coming all these miles. I'm crazy about you. And — I know you've been through a lot. If I were being logical, this is probably the absolute worst time to be pouring my heart out to you. But, I can't sleep and I can't think straight without knowing where I stand with you. I miss what we had on Harbour Island."

She watched as he took every breath, seemingly trying to maintain his composure. Several moments of her life flashed through her mind like a movie reel — the moment she knocked on Liam's hotel door, the moment he stood at her closet door with pride, the moment she packed her bags, and the moment she first laid eyes on Chuck.

Chuck reached for an envelope. "Like I said. My timing is probably terrible. And, for all I know I could've been misreading the whole thing. Either way, I'm going to give you some time to think things over," he said, passing her the envelope. "I'll be in town for a day. If interested, I got this for you. If not, no pressure to respond."

He placed the envelope in her hand, then proceeded to pass her by, heading for the door. Every fiber of her being wanted to turn the moment around. However, fear silenced the voice stirring on the inside leaving her feeling helpless. What if accepting Chuck's invitation to love would end just as horribly as her marriage had to Liam? What if this was her fate?

"Chuck," she said, in a faint voice. But the look on her face must've said a thousand words.

"Take your time, Nora. You know how to find me."

She watched as the door closed.

You can't let him go., she thought. But, the one person who needed to hear her profession of love was gone.

Nora opened the envelope and pulled out a round trip ticket with a destination to Nassau, Bahamas. A note attached read 'come away with me and relive the magic that brought us together.'

A tear fell down Nora's cheek, leading her to open the door and follow the prompting of her heart. "Chuck, wait."

Chapter 19

Epilogue

Chuck heard the sound of Nora's voice calling out and could recognize it from just about anywhere. But, on this particular morning, standing smack dab in the middle of Times Square, it was the most beautiful sound he'd ever heard. A moment he wouldn't forget for a long time to come.

He turned around. "Whoa. Slow down, there." He chuckled. "I'm right here... in town for another day, remember?"

He gently grasped her arms while she tried to catch her breath.

"Yes, but. I didn't want to wait for another day to go by. I wanted to respond to you now."

With a smile he replied, "Ah, you must've seen the tickets."

"Chuck, listen to me. With or without the tickets, you need to know that I feel the same way. Sure, am I afraid to dive into something new while I'm still fresh off the heels of —"

He placed a finger over her lips. "Shhh, I understand. You don't have to spell everything out here in public. I get it."

Nora looked around, then glanced into his eyes. "I really

don't care who hears me. When the man you're falling for walks into the studio while you're live on air to profess his feelings — you pay attention and you respond!" She looked at the envelope, then handed it to him. "And, you let him know that even if he didn't buy her roses or tickets to the islands, that you'd still want to be with him, no matter what."

Feeling certain that he was revealing his dimples, he said. "Oh, so. Does this mean you don't want to go back to Harbour Island with me?"

Chuck could feel himself smiling so hard he could barely keep it together. It was nice knowing that even when he threw logic out the window, his heart hadn't led him astray.

"No, silly. Of course, I want to go back to Harbour Island with you, but I want you more."

Well, I'll be damned, he thought. *Love truly is for people of all ages.*

"Nora Hutchins, I'd love nothing more than to take the trip of a lifetime with you, but I'd be honored if we could start with Harbour Island," he said, drawing her closer.

"Well, it sounds like we're getting off to a mighty good start, then. I guess you'll have to call Parker and Meg and tell them we're heading back."

In the middle of Times Square, Nora planted the sweetest long-lasting kiss Chuck had ever experienced. Even the flashing lights of nearby paparazzi couldn't stop the electrical surge that existed between them.

When they came up for air Chuck responded, "Yeah, so Parker and Meg kind of already have a heads up if you will."

Nora's eyebrows folded. "How so?"

"Well, let's just say that Parker was responsible for putting in a phone call to the right people who would help me to get in and see you."

With a burst of laughter, Nora replied, "Oh, really. So that's how you made it past security!"

"Well, who else could speak of your recent whereabouts and our connection other than the owner of the B&B? Hey, that's all I could come up with, but it worked!" he said.

"Indeed, it did. I'd normally have a chat with the crew for pulling a stunt like that, but I guess there's no need because I'm a free agent."

Chuck admired her rose colored cheeks and whispered softly, "You're my free agent."

Nora traced her finger along his lips. "And, you're mine."

* * *

While strolling down the avenue hand in hand, Nora turned to Chuck. "I don't think you ever got around to telling me the story about the original owners of the B&B."

"Ah, Old Man Barnes and his wife, Evelyn. Yes, they were a match made in heaven. They hosted people from around the world who enjoyed her fine cuisine and their overwhelming knack for making people feel at home. Sadly, she fell ill. Legend has it that Old Man Barnes hired help to keep the place going for a while. He mainly did it in honor of his wife. Slowly but surely he started running low on funds when his health started deteriorating. Years later he became ill and died." Chuck held up a finger. "But he didn't pass before offering a generous opportunity to Parker to become the next owner. And, I gladly take responsibility for making the connection between the two."

"Oh, wow, that's amazing," she said.

"Thank you. I knew Parker was the man for the job. And, now with his wife, Meg, they make the perfect team to carry on the legacy that Barnes and his wife left behind. There's something wonderful about that place. I can't quite put my finger on it, but I know it led me to you."

Nora stopped in her tracks. "It led us to each other."

Once again, the surrounding hustle and bustle of the city and all its sirens meant nothing to Nora and Chuck as they kissed. They were already standing in the midst of something greater — a powerful force called love.

New Tropical Breeze Series!

Can she find love when she's healing from heartache?

After a painful end to a long engagement, all Meg wants out of life is a fresh start.

She can't think of a better way to begin than by advancing her career in the hotel industry. When an opportunity comes along to accept a position at a five-star resort, she secures a beach house, packs her bags, and heads to the Bahamas.

But her oasis has been sold in an auction and the new owner and heartthrob, Parker Wilson, has no intention of holding onto a contract.

She'll have nowhere to stay, nowhere to heal, nowhere to grow if she gives in to his flippant attitude about her future.

When Meg digs her heels in and refuses to leave, will this drive them further into the arena of enemies? Or will they find common ground and potentially become lovers?

Tropical Encounter is a clean beach read with a splash of romance that's sure to give you all the feels.

Pull up your favorite beach chair and watch as Meg and Parker's story unfolds!

<u>Tropical Breeze Series:</u>
    Tropical Encounter: Book 1
    Tropical Escape: Book 2
    Tropical Moonlight: Book 3
    Tropical Summer: Book 4
    There's more to come!

Solomons Island Series

She's single, out of a job, and has a week to decide what to do with her life.

He lost his fiancé to a fatal accident while serving in the coast guard.

Will a chance encounter lead Clara and Mike to find love?

Clara's boss, Joan Russell, was a wealthy owner of a beachfront mansion, who recently passed away. Joan's estranged family members have stepped in, eager to collect their inheritance and dismiss Clara of her duties.

With the clock winding down, will Clara find a job and make a new life for herself on Solomons Island? Will a chance encounter with Mike lead her to meet the man of her dreams? Or will Clara have to do the unthinkable and return home to a family who barely cares for her existence?

This women's divorce fiction book will definitely leave you wanting more! If you love women's fiction and clean romance, this series is for you. Embark on a journey of new beginnings and pick up your copy today!

<u>Solomons Island Series:</u>

Beachfront Inheritance: Book 1

Beachfront Promises: Book 2

Beachfront Embrace: Book 3

Beachfront Christmas: Book 4

Beachfront Memories: Book 5

Beachfront Secrets: Book 6

Pelican Beach Series

She's recently divorced. He's a widower. Will a chance encounter lead to true love?

If you like sweet romance about second chances then you'll love The Inn At Pelican Beach!

At the Inn, life is filled with the unexpected. Payton is left to pick up the pieces after her divorce is finalized. Seeking a fresh start, she returns to her home town in Pelican Beach.

Determined to move on with her life, she finds herself

caught up in the family business at The Inn. It may not be her passion, but anything is better than what her broken marriage had to offer. Payton doesn't wallow in her sorrows long before her opportunity at a second chance shows up. Is there room in her heart to love again? She'll soon find out!

In this first book of the Pelican Beach series, passion, renewed strength, and even a little sibling rivalry are just a few of the emotions that come to mind.

Visit The Inn and walk hand in hand with Payton as she heals and seeks to restore true love.

Get your copy of this clean romantic beach read today!

Pelican Beach Series:
The Inn at Pelican Beach: Book 1
Sunsets at Pelican Beach: Book 2
A Pelican Beach Affair: Book 3
Christmas at Pelican Beach: Book 4
Sunrise At Pelican Beach: Book 5

www.ingramcontent.com/pod-product-compliance
Lightning Source LLC
Chambersburg PA
CBHW070511200726
48293CB00007B/2476